Double O Stephen
and the
GHOSTLY REALM

Double O Stephen and the

GHOSTLY REALM

ANGELA AHN

tundra

Tundra Books, an imprint of Tundra Book Group,
a division of Penguin Random House of Canada Limited

Library and Archives Canada Cataloguing in Publication

Title: Double O Stephen and the ghostly realm / Angela Ahn.
Names: Ahn, Angela, author.
Identifiers: Canadiana (print) 20210351659 | Canadiana (ebook)
20210351667 | ISBN 9780735268272 (hardcover) |
ISBN 9780735268289 (EPUB)
Classification: LCC PS8601.H6 D68 2022 | DDC jC813/.6—dc23

Published simultaneously in the United States of America by
Tundra Books of Northern New York, an imprint of Tundra Book Group,
a division of Penguin Random House of Canada Limited

Library of Congress Control Number: 2021949234

Edited by Lynne Missen
Designed by Sophie Paas-Lang
The text was set in Adobe Caslon Pro.

Printed in the United States of America

www.penguinrandomhouse.ca

1st Printing

Penguin
Random House
TUNDRA BOOKS

CHAPTER 1

*B*lackbeard's *Vestige* **had been moored** at Riverside Docks for about a week. I peeked in between two slats in the blinds covering my bedroom window to make sure it was still there. It was pretty awesome to look at all the different kinds of ships in the marina on a normal day, but now there was a *pirate ship* anchored practically right outside my room. How lucky could I get?

Just the sight of that ship changed this boring Monday morning in Cedar Coast into something special. The sun seemed to shine extra bright today, and though it was still early, people were out and about, starting their day.

Standing by my window, I realized I was still clutching my tattered copy of *Treasure Island*, and I put it down on my bedside table in its usual spot, next to the only other things that I kept there: my alarm clock and my lamp (lampshade with skull and cross-bones, of course).

The framed picture of me and Dad in our matching pirate outfits from last Halloween used to be on the table too, but I noticed that every time Mom came into my room and saw it, her eyes always began to bulge. I moved the picture into the table's small drawer so she wouldn't get permanent eye damage.

Blackbeard's Vestige was a small two-masted brigantine of no more than forty feet, and even from my tenth-floor condo, I could see that nobody had swabbed the deck for a very long time. The rails were crusted with bird poop, and the part of the hull that was out of the water sure could have used a fresh coat of paint. The canvas sails were rolled up tight against the booms, and at some point they had probably been white but you couldn't tell because of the thick grime, so they just looked sort of hazy.

The ship moored in the slip next to *Blackbeard's Vestige* was a Yacht with a capital *Y*. It was a real beauty. Sleek, chrome plating everywhere, and it looked like it could cut through the water like a knife through butter. Riding on that yacht would probably be fun, but if I could have my pick, I would choose *Blackbeard's Vestige* every single time. There is no finer vessel than a pirate ship if adventure and surprises are what you're after. It's a fact.

The deck of *Blackbeard's Vestige* showed no signs of life, except for the seagull that was perched atop the crow's nest on the main staff. The ship's Jolly Roger flapped steadily in the wind, indicating a Beaufort wind force scale of at least 4 (gentle breeze, 11 to 16 knots).

The Jolly Roger was an exact replica of the flag sailed on *Queen Anne's Revenge* by Blackbeard — the most notorious pirate to ever sail the seas. Set against a black background was a white demonic skeleton stabbing a bright-red bleeding heart. This image tingles my spine. Most people assume that Blackbeard was murderous and cruel, but actually he didn't like violence. He used his reputation to his advantage, and sometimes ships surrendered to him without a fight because the very *thought* of Blackbeard was enough. It was the ultimate flex.

"What are you doing?" It was Mom.

I whipped around. The blinds clattered loudly, and I looked at her dressed in her dark navy suit, ready to go to work. If I gave lectures about books all day like she did, I would wear track pants and a hoodie, but Minah Oh, the professor, liked to look "professional" at the university and always wore a dark suit that could have easily transitioned from the workplace to a funeral.

"Um . . ." I stumbled, grasping for the right words.

My mother came over to the window and twirled the wand attached to the blinds, slowly lifting the slats and letting sunlight gradually seep into the room. Her straight dark hair, cut in a perfect swoop across the back of her shoulders, caught the light, and for a second it almost looked like she wore a shimmering crown.

"What *are* you looking at?" she asked.

I shrugged my shoulders and decided to stay quiet. The truth was, I had caught a glimpse of some movement on the deck of *Blackbeard's Vestige* yesterday, and I had constantly been looking out the window since. I was convinced that it had been the captain. Surely a man who sailed a ship like *that* was a pirate. He had to be. If only I could meet him one day. Maybe he'd offer to be my mentor. Maybe he could teach me how to sail. Maybe he'd hurl insults at me. Even that would be okay. But first, I just needed a good look at him.

If you look up *pirate* in any dictionary, it seems like a simple concept. They'll give a definition like this:

> **PIRATES** are sailors who attack other ships and steal property from them.

No, no, no. I object! That's not right. A pirate is *so* much more. At the heart, a pirate is a courageous explorer and a bold adventurer who loves the sea — I like *that* part about them. That's the part that all the dictionary definitions don't capture. Why did they have to focus on the *stealing* part so much?

That's why the world needs a new word, a better word. Ready?

PIVENTURATE.

That's a word I made up myself. I can't get anybody else, except Brandon, to use it, though.

It's not hard to pronounce.

- *Pie*, like, you know, the delicious dessert
- *Ven*, like *vent* with no *t*
- *Chur*, like *churro*, another delicious dessert, but with no *o*, and
- *Rat*, like the rodent

Pie-ven-chur-rat.

Piventurates are sailors who passionately seek adventure. People who boldly travel into the unknown to explore and learn.

It's good, right? Names matter and *piventurate* definitely belongs in the dictionary, but so far, my email to Merriam-Webster had gone unanswered. The editors must get a lot of suggestions about adding new words to their text. I'll give them another week to respond before following up.

So, when I thought about the captain of *Blackbeard's Vestige*, I really hoped he was more along the lines of a piventurate, not a thieving marauder.

I have to be careful using my brilliant word around Mom, though. She quietly rolls her eyes whenever I say it. I've seen it a few times. Just to humor the ignorant types around me, I usually stick to *pirate*, even though I feel that the word is just totally inadequate. I had better try emailing the *Oxford Dictionary* people next.

"We need to leave in five minutes," Mom reminded me as we left my room. Her eyes darted to the wall clock in the hallway. "Or, if you'd like, you could ride your bike by yourself. I suppose you are old enough."

Finally, my first crack at some independence!

Twelve years of being smothered by her, and her anti-piventurate ways, was starting to get to me.

"Maybe just leave the bandanna at home?" she said hopefully, over her shoulder. Her face pinched slightly as her eyes crept up to the red bandanna I always wore on my head. "I bought you a nice ball cap the other day."

"Nah, I'm good," I told her as I gave the knot at the base of my neck a good tug. I slid into my favorite pair of red Crocs.

Her shoulders slumped slightly, but she quickly resumed getting ready. To make room for the large stack of student papers she was holding, she pushed the small framed black-and-white photograph of her mother, my grandma, to the back of the hallway table. As far as I knew, it was the only picture we had of her, because she had died a long time ago, before Mom had even come to Cedar Coast.

Can you believe she still requires students to submit on *paper*? Save a tree, Mom: Go digital. I caught a glimpse of the essay on the top of the stack, and it was covered with red circles and slashes. The student probably wouldn't be too thrilled with the C-.

Mom gave herself a quick glance in the small mirror on the wall and touched up her lipstick. She gathered the stack of papers into one hand and slid them into her leather briefcase.

Why did she take so long? I was ready ages ago. She finally slipped into her tight, shiny high-heeled shoes that made a *clack-clack* sound on the concrete of the underground parkade of our condo building.

"I'll walk home with Brandon, okay?" I flung my backpack over my shoulder.

"That's fine," she said. Her mouth looked puckered, but she didn't hold that face for very long because a faint clanging came from somewhere inside the apartment and drew her attention.

It sounded like metal being struck.

"What's that noise?" I listened closely.

Mom had this very serious look on her face. Her eyes seemed far away, like she was concentrating very carefully.

"Probably just the building's pipes," she finally said. She stared at the photo of Grandma and slid it back into its usual place.

"But it sounds like it's coming from inside *here* somewhere."

"Stephen, never mind, it's probably nothing. We're going to be late. Grab your ..." Then something else caught her attention. "Why is your jacket like this?" She took a step toward the coatrack on the other side of the front door.

I froze. It was one of those moments when I wished I could go back in time. Yesterday when I'd come home, I should have put my jacket away nicely, by hanging it up by its hood. Instead, I had tossed it up in the air and it managed to catch on to one of the other jackets, and it just stayed there. It *was* technically on a hook, not on the floor. At the time, it had seemed fine, but this morning I realized my mistake — the pocket wasn't fully zipped. I could see *it* was going to fall out.

I watched with building dread as Mom lifted my wrinkled jacket and gave it a good shake. She dislikes wrinkles a lot. Do you know anybody who irons their kitchen towels? I do.

My black eyepatch tumbled to the floor.

Instead of just staring at it lying there on the tile like a dead squirrel, I forced myself to steal a glance at my mother. She hated the bandanna, that was clear, but the eyepatch — well, that was next-level loathing. Last week, she had caught me wearing one in front of the bathroom mirror, and though my mother doesn't yell, she does have that pretty obvious eyeball bulging problem. That eyepatch was confiscated. For all I knew, she had thrown it away. But she didn't really think I only had *one*, did she?

"What. Is. This?" Each word was said slowly. She clenched the patch in her right hand.

"It's my backup," I said cautiously.

"I thought I told you that you were not to wear these in public." Her lips formed an angry donut.

"I don't! Just at recess and lunch! And only with Brandon."

"Oh, really, Stephen. Why?" she said with displeasure. Her calm demeanor cracked. "Why do you aspire to be a *pirate*?" She sighed deeply.

I wanted to remind her that I only say "pirate" because she and the rest of the world, especially dictionary editors, refused to acknowledge *piventurate* as a legitimate word, but instead I bit my tongue and hung my head. After all this time, she still didn't understand. Sometimes if you wanted to *be* something, you needed to dress the part.

"I rue the day your father decided to read *Treasure Island* to you!" she said, followed by a sharp breath inward. She covered her mouth with her hand while still holding the eyepatch.

I was shocked. "You said all books, no matter how poorly written, had some value!" I reminded her.

She looked embarrassed. "I spoke thoughtlessly. You're right. The book isn't to blame." Her eyelids closed heavily, and she did that thing she always does — she waved her hand across her face, like she was shooing a fly away. It was weird, because there wasn't ever a fly. "It's all your father's fault."

Mom liked to blame my dad, Christopher O'Driscoll, for everything. Climate change, the rising cost of fuel, their divorce, and especially my love of pirates — everything that was wrong with the world, or with me, was his fault.

Whenever she started talking about him, hives erupted on her neck.

She passed me my jacket and said, "I'm confiscating this one too!" I watched the eyepatch disappear into her briefcase. "Why do you have a seemingly endless supply of these?"

I kept quiet.

"Your father buys them, doesn't he?" Mom asked, snapping her spine up straighter. She continued to mutter to herself. "If only he hadn't taken you on his *friend's* boat, this would have all ended last year!"

It has been a total of three days since Mom last cursed Dad for taking me on a sailing trip down the coast with his girlfriend last year. At least *he* took me sailing *once* — which was one more time than Mom had. Daniela made me green smoothies for breakfast; it sounds worse than they tasted. The sensation of the saltwater pricking my cheeks and my shirt flapping in the wind as I sat on the starboard bench was a feeling I'd never forget.

The Climb was a fine-looking midsized pleasure boat, with a flybridge upper deck to catch the breeze but also a fully enclosed living and lounge space for when the seas were rough. I had really high hopes that one day Daniela would teach me to operate it, maybe even let me be the co-captain. The day I noticed that her Pilates machine wasn't in the spare room of Dad's townhouse was the day my piventurate heart was ripped out. But at least he still bought me pirate gear on the sly.

"Come on." Mom glanced at her watch. "We're going to be late." She suddenly looked very tired.

We both gathered our things and made our way out the front door. At the elevator in the middle of the hall-way, my mother reached for the "down" button. Using her finger like a jackhammer, she pressed it over and over again, as if pressing the button fifteen times in rapid succession would make the elevator come any faster.

"No more pirates, okay, Stephen?" Mom begged as we stepped inside the elevator.

"No more pirates," I muttered, just to keep her happy. *Piventurates, however, are another story,* I said to myself.

Slowly moving my right arm, I reached around to the zippered compartment at the top of my backpack and made sure that my homemade Jolly Roger was still there. Mom would really lose it if she found *that* — especially since I'd used one of her fancy dinner-party napkins to make it. The elevator doors closed, and I wondered if Brandon had a spare eyepatch in his backpack.

CHAPTER 2

We passed the lobby on our way to the parkade. A row of mailboxes lined one side of the room. On the tiled floor underneath the boxes was a plastic bag propped up against the wall with a piece of paper taped to it. It had a note on it, in Dad's handwriting. In big black letters: *Double O Stephen*.

Maybe you're wondering just what the heck that means. Well, my name is Stephen Oh-O'Driscoll. Yes, that is my actual full name. If you say anything about it, I'll make you walk the plank. Remember when I said that names mattered? Yes, it *mattered* to me that my name was ridiculous.

Many times, I've wondered what in the world they were thinking when they decided that this was a name that they were going to burden me with for the *rest of my life*. Just say it aloud to yourself once.

Did you do it? Then you must have come to the inevitable conclusion that the Korean last name *Oh* should never be hyphenated with the Irish last name *O'Driscoll*. Never. It just leaves the door wide open to a whole whack of nicknames — none of which I like.

I leaned down to pick up the bag and then opened it. Inside, a video game with a yellow sticky note attached to it: *Sorry, won't be able to take you this weekend. I've got an important client coming in. Have fun with the new game!* I peeled the note off and looked at the cover: *Battleships of Space*. Whoa! This game wasn't even out yet! Sometimes it is handy to have a dad who is a well-connected computer nerd.

"He's not taking you this weekend, I assume?" Mom asked.

"Something about a client coming in." I crumpled the note and threw it away in the bin next to the row of mailboxes. I shoved the game into my backpack.

"*Humph,*" she grunted.

"Does Dad ever buy you guilt gifts?" I asked. I thought about my secret stash of pirate gear hidden in a box in the bottom of my closet.

"Not once." She snorted. "Even when we were married."

Awkward. I hated it when she talked about their marriage in the past tense like that. But I guess it had been three years. Thank goodness we were at the bike lockers, and I could busy myself.

Mom watched me unlock the gate to the bicycle storage room and retrieve my bike. I shoved my helmet on over my bandanna, jamming it down hard. But it messed up my bandanna knot. Everything needed a readjustment.

"Gets in the way, doesn't it?" she asked.

I ignored her and brushed my hair back so I could start again. After I managed to fix everything, I told her, "Okay then, I guess I'll be off."

The chin strap pinched, but was I going to let her know that the bandanna actually *was* getting in the way? Nope.

"Have a good day." She leaned in to give me a limp side-hug. Then she brushed her hand over her jacket to smooth out the wrinkles.

Clack-clack. She walked to our car and started the engine. I waited for her to go first, because having been a passenger in her car, I knew it was best to stay out of her way. The wheels of the Camry let out a high-pitched squeal, and soon the car was out of sight. Don't let the business suit fool you — Mom was a speed demon.

I pushed my bike up the sloped driveway out of the building to the security gate and pressed the "exit" button. Riverside Docks was in the opposite direction of where I needed to go to get to school, but a little detour that gave me some extra exercise wouldn't be the worst thing, right?

My eyes should have been firmly glued to the bicycle path, but I couldn't help but glance over to *Blackbeard's Vestige*. I pulled my bike over to the locked gate at the top of the metal ramp that led down to the docks. From here, if I stood in just the right spot, I could see a bit of the port side of the boat's main deck.

I looked for a few moments before I saw him. Somebody was on the deck of *Blackbeard's Vestige*. My heart started to race. He was wearing a hat — a *baseball* hat. I felt a little swell of disappointment; it didn't seem very pirate-y, never mind piventurate-y. I couldn't see much else at first, because he seemed to be on his knees. Then I saw his hands. Leathery. Definitely seafaring hands. He was tying knots on a rope. When his head turned in my direction, I completely freaked out.

I don't know what came over me, but I dropped my bike like the handlebars were on fire and darted to the side. My spine was pressed up against the pillar of the gate door. I couldn't see down the metal ramp to the berths anymore, and I hoped that he couldn't see me either.

As a rusty bolt pressed into my back, I wondered what the heck was wrong with me. I had just seen the *captain* of the boat. This was the person I had been hoping to see for the past week! I hit myself on the side of my head so I'd snap out of it.

I let myself puff out a few short breaths before I gathered enough nerve to peel my back off the pillar and peek down the ramp again. But he was gone.

Suddenly, I felt like a fool. A fool that was going to be late for school. I had just missed my chance to meet the man I had been wanting to meet all week. I hopped back onto my bike and rode off, shaking my head at myself the entire way.

Several students jostled me as I made my way slowly into the cloakroom of my class. Isabel impatiently pushed past me. She was small but mighty.

"Come on, Stephen. Move," she said.

My legs were wobbly from riding hard.

"Sorry," I replied into my chest. I looked around for Brandon, but he wasn't here yet. He'd been walking to school by himself for over two years already, and it was pretty normal if he rushed in at the final bell.

"*Argh!*" James said into my ear, giving me his bad pirate impersonation. "It's Stephen Uh-Oh!" Here came the worst part — he formed circles with his fingers and put them around his eyes like binoculars. Like two *O*'s, get it?

I scrunched my nose to sneer at him. James came up with that nickname last year and hasn't stopped using it since. The first time he said it, I boiled inside for, like, a week. Then he added the hand gesture. Is there any wonder why I hate my name so much?

"Find any treasure this weekend?" he persisted. Today, he smelled like spaghetti and meatballs. It was hard to hate him as much as usual when he smelled so delicious.

Ms. Atwal saved my life by coming into the cloakroom and saying, "Come on! Put your things away quickly!" She ushered James away from me.

Almost everybody had settled into their desks by the time Brandon streaked into class, wearing a new T-shirt with a parrot dressed as a pirate on the front. My eyes lit up, and my mouth dropped open. Brandon dashed to his desk before the last bell, with only seconds to spare. He caught my eye, pointed to his T-shirt, and gave me a quick thumbs-up.

Ms. Atwal smiled at him as she held the attendance sheet in her hand. "Three seconds away from being marked late, Brandon." Her brown eyes sparkled at him.

"Then I'm two seconds early." He grinned his patented wide, bright smile.

Ms. Atwal threw her head back and laughed. I counted four fillings. "Okay, okay, Brandon. Take your seat. It's time for our Mindful Minute." Ms. Atwal turned off the lights.

I sat at my desk with my eyes closed. I was supposed to release all my thoughts, but instead I was wondering how Brandon did it. Just getting people to smile and laugh *with* him and not *at* him, like people did to me.

I started to squirm in my seat. This Mindful Minute sure was taking a long time.

"Okay." Ms. Atwal flicked the lights back on. "It's time to start our day!"

If I just focused on getting through the next hour and thirty-five minutes, it would be recess. At least Brandon and I could practice sword fighting during our breaks. We'd been caught once or twice lashing our sticks together, and the on-duty supervision aide would always warn us to stop, but we only stopped when we thought she was looking. We were getting pretty decent at our footwork (we'd watched a bunch of videos online) and also avoiding detection from adults.

But we weren't that great at the actual sword fighting part. Not yet, anyway. Last week, I poked a hole in Brandon's favorite T-shirt. He pretended that he wasn't upset at me, but I could tell he was having trouble smiling after it happened. Then the time he slashed my forearm, leaving a welt — well, I wasn't too happy about that either. But we both knew that being a piventurate in training was pretty serious business, and of course there were going to be some cuts and bruises. It just wasn't fun when your arm throbbed for the rest of the afternoon.

Today, when recess finally rolled around, I asked Brandon, "Where did you get that T-shirt?" I figured he'd got it to make up for the hole I'd made in the other one.

"My dad ordered it online for me!"

"Nice," I told him, but my stomach clenched. I could never imagine Mom ordering *me* a T-shirt like that. Dad would, though. I'd drop a hint next time I saw him.

"Do you have an extra eyepatch?" I asked.

"Of course!" He reached into the small zippered compartment on the front of his bag. He handed me one and then put his in his jacket pocket. "You forgot yours?"

"I didn't forget. She found it."

Brandon looked at me sympathetically. "Oh, dang."

"Tell me about it. Come on!" The classroom had already started to clear.

We raced to our favorite spot in the woods next to the school as quickly as we could. Recess was only twenty minutes long and it sometimes passed in the blink of an eye. Today's late-spring weather was perfect, and I wanted to use every second of our free time.

The small wooded area was dense with trees and shrubs. It wasn't as popular a hang-out spot as it used to be because the school had built a new playground this year. Hardly anybody came by anymore and that suited me just fine. Brandon and I stopped when we reached the small clearing underneath a big old fir tree that constantly dropped twigs under its canopy.

"Why are there no sticks today?" Brandon said, throwing up his hands in frustration.

I frowned. The seconds were ticking away.

"Over there." I pointed to a scrubby bush with some twigs sticking out of it.

"They look big." He walked up to the bush and wrestled a small branch out of the thorny mess.

The stick was bigger than we were used to. The fir tree only dropped pieces about a foot long and usually quite thin. Brandon was holding a branch that was at least an inch in diameter and three feet long. He passed it to me. The bark was rough and full of knobby bumps over its entire length. He continued to hunt around until he pulled out another one, even thicker and just as coarse as mine.

He looked at the second branch suspiciously, tossing it back and forth between his hands. "What do you think? Seems fine."

We had wasted over half of recess already. "It's probably okay?" I ventured. "They do seem a bit heavy..."

"Are we training or are we complaining?" Brandon asked. His face perked up. "Oh, that's a good one. I'm using it again."

My fist closed around the branch tightly, still not quite sure.

"We've been working up to more, haven't we? Practicing a lot, right?" Brandon insisted.

"Okay. Let's give it a go," I said. I knew we only had a few minutes of recess left.

Tucking the branch under his armpit, Brandon reached into his pocket and pulled out his eyepatch. Pulling the elastic strap over his head of brown curls, he affixed the patch over his left eye.

I did the same. Brandon's eyepatch fit nicely over my bandanna, and I gave everything a final adjustment before I was ready. I nodded at Brandon, and he nodded back.

Using two hands, we held our sticks tight to our chests, pointed upward. We stood back-to-back. The noise of the other students in the surrounding fields melted away. It was just us.

"Are you ready?" I asked.

"Aye." Brandon's mood changed. A seriousness enveloped him, and I could hear him take a deep breath.

"The Piventurate's Oath," I said.

We both recited it at the same time.

We draw no blood
We play as one
We never give up
'Cause quitting's no fun
We keep our word
We are best mates
Piventurates for life
Adventure is our fate

"Begin," Brandon said.

We took three long, exaggerated steps apart and then swiveled on our heels to face each other.

The heavier stick made me unsure on my feet. It was almost like wielding a gnarled broom handle. I tried to parry, like I could with the smaller twigs we usually used, but this branch was too heavy to hold with one hand for very long. I had to switch to a two-handed sword grip. My feet were set — right foot slightly ahead and left foot behind for balance.

I watched Brandon struggle as he adjusted the grip on his heavier branch. Finally, feeling like I had a steady body position, I lifted my branch above my head, and I unleashed a strike. The speed of the strike surprised me.

It must have surprised Brandon too because he lifted his branch to block me, but the block was slow. Our branches clashed low, at chest level. The rough bits of bark on both branches caught awkwardly against themselves, and just as Brandon pulled his branch down away from mine, I yanked up. The branches snagged, just for a fraction of a second, and my smaller branch curved slightly because of the tension. When the branches finally released, the tip of mine sprang back at Brandon's face. It smashed directly into his open mouth.

"Ow!" he wailed. His hand flew up to his face, and his branch clattered to the ground.

I immediately dropped mine too and rushed over to Brandon. He was hunched over. I felt sick to my stomach.

"Oh my gosh, Brandon! Are you okay?" I leaned over to get a good look at him, but he was still bent over, staring at the ground. His hands were on his knees, like he was trying to catch his breath.

"At least you drew no blood." Then he stood up straight and flashed his smile. His two front teeth were chipped.

CHAPTER 3

Sitting on the hard wooden chair outside the principal's office was worse than playing dodgeball in PE. I would have given anything to be standing in the gym while rubber balls pelted me from every direction.

Instead, I was sitting here, waiting for my mother.

"Stephen," Brandon whispered. He sat on the bench a few feet away. The bench was the "I'm waiting to get picked up" spot. My wooden chair was the "I'm in trouble" spot.

I picked my chin off my chest and slowly looked at him. I thought he must be furious. He'd probably not want to be my friend anymore.

Instead, he grinned and then stuck his tongue out of the gap where his front teeth used to be. They weren't nice little white squares anymore. Instead, he had two triangles, like sharp little fangs, with just enough space between for him to squeeze the tip of his tongue through.

Brandon gave a silent chuckle. His eyepatch had been pushed up onto his forehead, and I remembered that I still had the eyepatch I had been wearing in my hand. Silently, I leaned out of my chair and passed it to him. I definitely did not want my mother seeing me holding it.

I forced myself to smile back at him, but I was feeling wretched. I don't know how he managed to find this situation funny, but he did. His teeth were wrecked because of *me*.

Brandon's mom waddled into the office. That baby was going to pop out any day now.

"Brandon!" Mrs. Markovich looked slightly frazzled as she squatted uncomfortably to look at him. The belt of her trench coat was just about to fall out of its loop around her waist, but she looked like she really didn't care. "Let me see!" She cradled his chin in her hands.

Keeping his teeth locked, he smiled at her with just his lips open in an exaggerated way.

"Your beautiful teeth!" she gasped.

"It was just an accident," he told her.

"Okay, okay, Joan, breathe. Just like in class," Mrs. Markovich told herself. Her eyes were shut. "Release the tension. Find your center." She spoke quietly as she pushed the palms of her hands down in front of her large belly, like she was pressing the air. But her breath sounded quaky, and it appeared she was unable to release her tension or find her center.

Mr. Huntington stepped out of his office and greeted Mrs. Markovich.

"Yes, we had an unfortunate incident at recess today, didn't we, Brandon?"

"It was an accident," he repeated. "Stuff happens. When you're training, there's no complaining." He shot me a look and raised his eyebrows quickly.

I smacked my forehead.

"What exactly *did* happen?" Mrs. Markovich demanded. She did her loud, ragged breathing again while struggling to stand. Brandon put a hand under her armpit to help her up.

"Stephen, would you like to explain?" Mr. Huntington turned to me.

Now would have been a very poor time to say no, so instead I glanced at him, swallowed hard, and opened my mouth to try to speak, but my tongue froze.

I heard the distinctive *clack-clack* of my mother's shoes from down the hall. Suddenly, I broke out into a cold sweat.

She emerged through the door of the office with her jaw firm and tense. I only held her gaze for a second before I looked at the ground.

"Mrs. Oh," Mr. Huntington said.

I cringed. He had said the forbidden word.

"Pardon me, it's *Doctor* Oh," Mom corrected him.

To call my mother "Mrs." was to take one step closer to your own demise. Dr. Oh sounded like the name of a fake doctor on an infomercial or a Marvel villain, but that was what she liked. I sighed heavily.

Mr. Huntington usually seemed like a strong man. He was well over six feet tall and towered over my small Korean mother, but with one sentence, it was like she had taken a longsword and viciously cut him down at his knees.

He cleared his throat and said, "Stephen was just about to tell us what happened."

I nervously looked at Brandon, who stuck his tongue through the hole between his teeth again. He was handling the damage surprisingly well. On the other hand, I was feeling violently ill.

"We were just playing," I managed to finally say.

"Playing what?" Mom pressed.

I fell silent again.

"Tag!" Brandon spoke up and lied loudly.

Mom turned quickly to stare at him. He held her gaze for a surprisingly long time before he reached to the top of his head and slowly took off the eyepatch.

"Tag indeed," Mom said as she peered down her nose. "Stephen, were you two playing pirates? I demand to know the truth."

"Yes," I squeaked. I felt like a mouse, and I sounded like one too.

"It's piventurate training!" Brandon stood up. "How can we ever get good at sword fighting if we never practice? We need to develop our skill set!"

I wanted to disappear into my seat.

"Your poor, perfect teeth," Mrs. Markovich lamented with her fingers pressed deep into her temples. She had given up her slow breathing and was close to hyperventilating.

"I have a few things I need to discuss with Mrs., uh, *Doctor* Oh," Mr. Huntington told Mrs. Markovich. "You will probably want to take Brandon to the dentist?"

"Yes, yes." Mrs. Markovich looked bewildered. "Come on, Brandon."

"I'm sorry," I whispered as they began to leave.

Brandon looked back and gave me the quickest of waves before he disappeared down the hall.

Mr. Huntington gestured for us to come into the office, and when the door latched behind us, my heart sank.

"Stephen will be suspended for three days." He hadn't even sat down in his chair yet before dropping the bomb.

"Three days?" Mom exclaimed.

"Firstly, he has been warned about using sticks as weapons on previous occasions."

Okay, I had to admit he was right about that one. I sulked.

"Secondly, he has caused bodily harm to another student."

I chipped my best friend's teeth by *accident*. Did he really think it was on purpose? It happened because I was inadequately trained in sword fighting, not because I had violent tendencies. I felt bad enough about it without being punished even more. Why was nobody paying attention to me?

"Third." He paused. "He is in breach of the school's dress code by continuously wearing a head covering that is clearly not faith-based in nature."

Wrong! Being a piventurate was like my religion. Mr. Huntington had crossed a line. A big line. I wanted so badly to stand up and defend myself, defend my bandanna, defend the right to train as a piventurate, but all I could manage was an angry huff.

At least it didn't sound like Brandon was going to be punished on top of everything else. Emergency dental work was punishment enough.

Mom shifted slightly in her seat. "I find your reasoning highly subjective, but I suppose you are enjoying your small moment of perceived power. However, I must admit that I do agree with your position on the head covering."

My mouth dropped and I turned to look at her. If I didn't know her better, I would have sworn she was smirking, but since my mother doesn't have a sense of humor, it might have been gas.

Mom pushed back her chair and stood, while Mr. Huntington remained seated. Our eyes finally met, and she jerked her head to the door. She had sounded so fierce and daunting — until she had *agreed* with Mr. Huntington. Traitor! They were both just pouring salt in my wound. Brandon was off to the dentist because of me. Did they need to keep reminding me of my mistake?

"When you return to school on Friday, Stephen, it will be *without* the bandanna," Mr. Huntington said, raising his voice as we walked out of his office.

I tried to turn around to look at him, to tell him that I'd heard him, but I found I couldn't do it. Instead, I ripped my bandanna off my head and shuffled away.

CHAPTER 4

"**T**oday is museum day," Mom announced over breakfast on the first day of my suspension.

Museum day? Why was she like this? I had hoped today would be the day I cracked open *Battleships of Space*, but I rarely got what I wanted.

Her eyes glued to her laptop, Mom said, "The Museum of Cedar Coast has an exhibition called *Rewilding the Urban Landscape*. Sounds like a nice examination of the issue of balancing population density with the creative incorporation of green spaces."

Huh?

"I'm making up for your school's ineffectiveness." Mom looked up from the screen. "I've had to reschedule my seminars, most unprofessional, and if I must be home, we shall do our best to have an informative day."

"I could have stayed home by myself," I finally said after swallowing my last bit of toast. *Battleships of Space* would have been *informative* enough for me.

"I'm sure if Mr. Huntington caught wind of *that*, he'd send an appropriate government agency after me."

I had to agree. He seemed like the vindictive kind.

"Have you spoken to your friend?" she asked casually.

"Brandon?"

"His teeth. Have they been . . . repaired?" She resumed looking at her screen.

"I don't know," I admitted. I had not been feeling great about the whole thing and I had been too scared to check in with him yesterday.

"*Hmm*," she replied vaguely. "I have a few emails to answer, and the museum doesn't open until ten thirty. You have plenty of time to complete your homework before we leave." Her fingers started flying over the keyboard.

"Uh, sure."

I put my plate away in the dishwasher and went to my room. My computer was in sleep mode, so I jiggled my mouse to wake it up. The first thing that popped up on the screen was the notification that Brandon had messaged me last night, but I had missed it.

> Check out these temporary babies.

He had included a close-up photo of his teeth. The temporary ones seemed to shine extra bright. I let out a breath of relief and found myself smiling. He'd probably be rushing into school right now and wouldn't see my reply, but I sent it anyway.

> Awesome. 👍 Plus, sorry.

He sent me a reply immediately.

> No prob C U when I C U. 😜

> Aren't u LATE?

> Aaaaaaah!!!!

I laughed with relief. While staring at my ceiling last night feeling sorry for myself, I had been scared that maybe he wouldn't forgive me this time. I wouldn't be at school for a few days, but now I knew that when I returned, things would be back to normal.

I swiveled at my desk and pushed my chair toward the window. The room was dark and needed some light. I pulled the cord on the blinds, and the slats zipped up to the top of the window.

Blackbeard's Vestige was gone! My heart sank like an anchor. Maybe that was why the captain was tying up ropes when I saw him yesterday. He was preparing to head out on a piventurate expedition and hoist the sails. I, on the other hand, was going to a museum with my mother. Yippee.

Recalling how I had behaved yesterday at the gate of the marina made me want to hurl up my toast. Why hadn't I just *looked* at him? Why had I hidden like that? Now that the boat was gone, who knew how long it would be until I would have the chance to see him again.

I turned my back to the window — the view was still good but not nearly as interesting anymore. There were other things that needed my attention, and homework wasn't one of them. I quietly opened the top drawer of my nightstand and pulled out my Jolly Roger, which I had folded up and placed on top of the photo of me and Dad from last Halloween.

Many Sharpie markers had been sacrificed to transform the white napkin into a black flag, but finally I was almost done. Just as I uncapped a marker, I heard the annoying clanging sound again.

Still sitting at my desk, I rolled my desk chair over to my bedroom door and stuck my head out into the hallway. I caught a brief glimpse of Mom quietly dashing into her room. Definitely the same noise as yesterday. Was our condo building falling apart?

I headed to Mom's room just to make sure there wasn't a burst pipe or anything. Last month, a neighbor's toilet had leaked and the apartment below them had flooded. They had to move out for two weeks.

The clanging was still a bit muffled, and I put my ear up to the wall in the hallway, just outside Mom's room. It sounded as if it was coming from close by. I braced myself for an expected rush of toilet water.

Mom's door was closed but not shut tight. I pushed it open and she was standing with her back to me, in front of her closet, holding onto something.

"Hey, do you hear the clanging?" I asked.

She jumped a little and her head snapped back to look at me.

"Oh, you scared me," she said breathlessly.

"What are you doing?"

"Nothing." She reached for the closet door, opened it slightly, and dropped the item she was holding back inside.

"What was that?" I had just caught a glimpse of the object. It looked kind of like a metal plate.

She puckered her lips. "I was just doing some research."

I scrunched my eyebrows. The clanging seemed to have a smothered sound to it, as if the insulation in the walls were dampening it.

"I'd better call the building maintenance about that noise!" She reached for the phone on her bedside table. "I'd like some privacy, please." Instead of dialing right away, she held the phone tightly in her left hand.

"Okay," I said, feeling generally confused.

I stepped out of her room and closed the door behind me. After two steps, I stuck my ear up against the wall again. The clanging had stopped, and I could hear her talking to somebody, almost yelling into the phone. I headed back to my room so I could get back to work on my Jolly Roger.

With the background done, it was time to think about the design. I wasn't about to put a skeleton on mine like Blackbeard's had — that wasn't like me at all. But I did have a couple of cool ideas. There were things that were important to me and needed to be on my flag.

We drove to a really pretty spot on the edge of Sunrise Beach Park. From here you could see the entire harbor. The water was choppy, with small whitecaps cresting on the surface, the sky was clear, and it would have been a perfect day to be out for a jaunt. Not that I would ever tell Mom, but sometimes I looked out and wondered if Dad's ex, Daniela, was sitting on the prow of *The Climb*, enjoying a bowl of something very healthy.

As she parked the car, I counted at least ten vessels in and around the coastline, and I couldn't help but feel satisfied with the view. Some were small craft, like cat rigs with only one sail, less than thirty feet in length; but there were also larger sloops, at least fifty feet long. Though from here, it was hard to guess sizes correctly.

We got out of the car, and I recognized the building. I told Mom, "Oh, I came here on a field trip last year or maybe the year before, remember?"

"I'm sure you didn't see everything. They change the exhibits regularly. There is always plenty to learn." She started to walk quickly to the front door.

Sometimes Mom was too busy learning to be really living. I jogged up the curved ramp to catch up.

They had just opened and there was nobody else there.

After Mom paid the entrance fee, the young woman at the ticket booth, Margo, held out a pamphlet.

"We just turned over our exhibits today. We are featuring *The Famous and the Infamous: An Eclectic History of Cedar Coast*. Here's a map and brief guide to the displays."

Mom bristled. "But your website said that the exhibit was *Rewilding the Urban Landscape*! There's a giant sign out front!" She turned and pointed in its general direction.

"I'm sorry. As I said, it just turned over today. The facilities crew haven't changed the sign yet or updated the website," Margo said with a shrug. She crinkled her nose and pushed up her glasses with her free hand.

Mom paused and her face turned into something resembling a large prune before she asked, "Can I get my money back?"

Her sudden change of heart was surprising.

"It's okay, Mom, I don't mind seeing it. We're here anyway. What's the big deal?" I mean, I really didn't care whether we stayed or left, but I did mind Mom behaving in a humiliating way. You don't just pay for an entrance ticket and then suddenly change your mind.

She waved her hand furiously across her face. Now add that weird thing she always does, and this was just getting worse by the second.

"Mom," I begged. I turned my body slightly so Margo couldn't see my desperate, pleading eyes.

"I was just not expecting this. I would not have brought you here had I known the exhibit was about the famous and infamous from Cedar Coast's history!"

Wow, she must have really been excited to see *Rewilding the Urban Landscape*.

Margo was still holding the pamphlet in the air, with her mouth slightly open.

"Sorry you're disappointed. The best I can do is offer you two complimentary vouchers for your next visit." She added two preprinted tickets on top of the pamphlet.

Mom took a sharp, quick breath. "Fine, but next time, please change your website and your signage to accurately reflect the current exhibit. Most unprofessional!" She snatched the brochure and the free tickets and roughly shoved them into her purse. Almost immediately, she took off like a rocket fueled by irritation to the doors that led to the exhibition rooms.

"I didn't know you were such a history hater, Mom." I struggled to catch up.

"I don't hate history, Stephen. I was simply . . . surprised." She faced forward and wouldn't look me in the eye.

CHAPTER 5

The Museum of Cedar Coast was small. The way the exhibit was laid out, it forced you to walk through the displays in a certain way. First, you went through a precolonial display, where there was a huge replica showing what the interior of a traditional Indigenous longhouse might have looked like. Plus, a wall with woven cedar-bark baskets and some wood carvings — the coolest one was a huge, brightly painted salmon.

Then the displays transitioned to a section entitled "Urban Legends." Before I read too much, I noticed a life-sized wax statue further along. The sign above it said "Just a shipwrecked merchant ship captain or a PIRATE?"

Anchors away! This museum had my full attention now!

I took a step closer to read the placard that was next to the statue.

Captain William J. Sapperton was born in Plymouth in 1846 into a seafaring family. Willy (as he preferred to be called) became a captain at the young age of twenty-five. His ship, *The Eidolon*, was commissioned primarily as a cargo ship. During a terrible storm in September of 1872, *The Eidolon* veered off course and Willy found himself in an inlet near what is known today as Cedar Coast. With a severely damaged ship and no way to return home, Willy, with a small number of crew, almost starved but learned how to fish the local waters with the help of Indigenous residents from a small village up the coast. Neither Willy nor his crew ever returned to England.

The district now known as Rail's End was the spot where the crew set to work clearing land and building modest dwellings. Willy earned his nickname, "Windy Willy," because he was always known to tell tales from the high seas that could keep an entire tavern on the edge of their seats in rapt attention.

On many occasions, he tried — unsuccessfully — to run for mayor of the growing community. Although many of the elections were closely contested, Willy never emerged as the winner. It is believed that rumors around his past may have resulted in his political downfall. Though Willy always denied the stories, there were persistent whispers that *The Eidolon* was not, and had never been, a "regular" cargo ship. In fact, during one mayoral election, the word PIRATE had been scrawled across the front door of his house before being hastily painted over.

Willy died a bachelor at the age of seventy-six.

Do you believe the rumors that Captain William J. Sapperton could have been a pirate?

I felt shaken. Having lived my whole life in Cedar Coast, I'd heard his name before — there is even a pancake restaurant named after him — but I hadn't really heard about the whole pirate angle. Could it really be true? I knew it wasn't good to believe rumors, but this rumor was one I *wanted* to believe.

I looked at the statue of Captain William J. Sapperton a little more closely.

Wax statues were creepy. Not real enough that you believed they were actual people, but real enough to be disturbing. He had a full dark beard and wore a floppy hat. His navy-blue jacket had a short front and long tails in the back. I liked how he held the lapels of his jacket. There was something amusing about it.

I stepped past the wax figure to look at another object that was placed on a pedestal nearby. It was an old wooden box that was rough around the edges with a lid that didn't fit quite right. The sign next to the box said "Sea Chest from *The Eidolon*." Wait, wait. Sea chest! That was just another word for *treasure chest*.

I mean, come on. That was practically like "*X* marks the spot." Was there any doubt? This dude was a pirate.

My heartbeat kicked into high gear. I stepped as close to the chest as I dared. The area was cordoned off with a thick velvety red rope, which obviously meant "Stay on the other side of this rope." Next to the box was a display of mannequins wearing old-fashioned clothes — men with top hats and suits with tails, and women in dresses made from patterned fabrics with lots of frills and lacey bits and full skirts.

The lid had been affixed with two iron hinges on the back of the box. On the front was a small rectangular brass plate engraved with Willy's name. A large keyhole sat just above the nameplate.

Standing there in front of the box, I had the strangest feeling. As though energy buzzed around me and *through* me.

I really don't know why I did it. I don't know where any good sense I may have had went to, but something was making me belly up to the rope — the rope meant to keep me away from the display. It stretched tight against my stomach.

My hand reached for the box. My index finger aimed directly at the nameplate. It was almost as though I couldn't *not* touch it. The tip of my finger traced the name *William J. Sapperton*.

As soon as I lifted my finger off the nameplate, a jolt radiated through it, down to my elbow. Like the worst case of electric shock I'd ever felt. Not as bad as a lightning bolt (I'd imagine) but definitely worse than a static shock from walking on a dry carpet.

I tried to shake the pain out of my hand. Then I heard her.

"You didn't." Mom's voice cut through the silence. Where had she been? I hadn't noticed her for the last few minutes.

"Do what?" I asked, dropping my hand to my side.

"You touched the box!" she exclaimed.

I was just about to give a half-hearted denial when I heard a quiet clinking noise. My head turned quickly. The nameplate that I had just touched had fallen off and hit the plastic of the pedestal before gently tumbling to the ground. It landed softly on the carpet. I froze.

Wrecking an antique in a museum was surprising enough, but even more unexpected was when Mom made a quick lunge at the display. Her right leg extended under the rope toward the nameplate on the floor. With a shocking amount of flexibility, she flicked her toe, and the small plate fluttered gently before landing underneath the hem of the dress on the mannequin a few feet away. The next thing I knew, Mom's hand was clamped over my wrist, and I was being dragged away.

Instead of following the exhibit to view the rest of the museum, we doubled back through the part we had already seen, which was hardly anything. Mom pushed through the doors, and I felt like a limp doll being dragged along. Her grip was tight, and my arm still felt tingly from the shock I had received earlier. As we passed Margo at the ticket desk, she stood up with her mouth open as if to say something, but Mom shot her free hand up in the air and gave her a firm look that basically said *Don't ask!* Margo closed her mouth and sat down.

Once we had exited the building, Mom finally let go of my hand.

My feet stopped moving and I found my voice. "What the heck was that?" I yelled. Mom pulled out the key fob to open the doors.

"Get in!" she said loudly without turning around.

The engine was already running before I even opened the passenger side door. I fastened my seat belt and turned to stare at her.

"Why are you acting so weird?" I asked.

She reversed the car and the tires squealed. But she didn't answer; she just kept driving.

"Why did you kick the nameplate? Shouldn't we have told somebody about it?" I pressed on.

Her eyes were affixed to the road. She took a deep breath and said very calmly, "I think the modern art gallery would be a much more pleasant way to spend the morning."

"So, you're just going to pretend that didn't happen?" I opened and closed my hand. The buzzy feeling was fading, and it was starting to feel normal again.

"I did what I felt was right," she replied.

"But . . . why?" I finally blurted out.

She glanced away from the road to look me square in the eyes. "I was trying to protect you."

"From the museum police?" I asked sarcastically.

She paused. "Yes, it wouldn't have been . . . professional . . . for you, as my son, to be known as a desecrator of local artifacts. My reputation at the university would have been ruined!"

Her reputation? I scoffed as I glared at her. This wasn't about her protecting *me* at all. Somehow, she was making it all about her. Typical. I shook my head and stared out the window.

CHAPTER 6

The "Closed for a Private Event" sign on the front door of the art gallery did nothing to improve Mom's mood.

I pressed my lips tight to prevent myself from saying something that might have been unfortunate.

"But I already paid for parking!" She was talking to the glass front door of the closed gallery, not me.

She continued to stare through it as if that was going to change things.

"Now what?" I dared to ask, glancing at my watch. Eleven twenty in the morning.

"Now what, indeed," Mom replied, the color drained from her face. "This day is going very poorly." She rubbed her forehead with her fingertips.

For a brief moment, everything went silent. The noise from traffic disappeared, and as my mother and I glanced at each other, my stomach growled loudly and unmistakably.

A deep wrinkle emerged between her eyebrows. Mom looked at her watch. "It's a bit early for lunch."

I disagreed and so did my stomach. Why was *brunch* reserved for weekends only? Now was the perfect time for a meal.

"Did you hear the ad on the radio on the drive here? There's a new restaurant — Ye Olde Pasta Warehouse — and they are having a grand opening lunch special. Six ninety-five for a pasta and a salad. Sounds pretty good, right?"

"Yes, very reasonable," Mom agreed. "The name of the restaurant, however, leaves something to be desired."

"Let's walk there," I suggested. "Since you already paid for parking."

"Where is it? I wasn't really paying attention to the radio."

"I think they said they had a location in Rail's End. It's not too far from here, right?"

Mom's face dropped. "Rail's End?"

"Yeah, Rail's End. Come on." I motioned with my head for us to leave. We had been standing in front of the art gallery doors for what seemed like forever.

"On second thought, Stephen, let's just stay around here." Mom gestured to the corner of Juniper and Century streets.

"Why?" I asked, confused.

"Oh, my feet hurt. I'm not sure I'm up to walking to Rail's End." Mom looked down at her flats with the very pointy toes. I'd seen her walk the entire length of the seawall around Riverside Docks in her high heels. Compared to the shoes she wore to work, these shoes looked way more comfortable. But then again, those pointy toes had also been sharp enough to flick the nameplate a couple of feet, so maybe they pinched. I eyed her and her shoes skeptically.

"Okay, it's fine. I'll get Dad to take me next time I see him," I told her. I really didn't feel like arguing. Maybe we'd finally just go home after lunch and then I could get started on *Battleships of Space*. "We can just get a burger or something." I pointed across the street to a row of fast-food restaurants.

At the mention of Dad, she started scratching her neck. She inhaled quickly. "No, I think I can do it."

Now I was really confused. She was usually decisive — her opinions were firm and solid. It was very out of character for her to flop around like a fish out of water. I tilted my head to the side. "Okay," I told her, not wanting to make a big deal out of it.

My first steps away from the gallery were tentative, and I waited for Mom to move. Did her shoes really bother her? She stood still for a few seconds before she waved her hand frantically across her face, and finally, she took a few quick steps to catch up to me before she bolted ahead in the direction of Rail's End.

Mom led us down streets that were not that familiar to me, so it kind of felt like I was being a tourist in Cedar Coast. That was when I noticed that the streets actually *were* full of tourists.

Several large luxury tour buses were parked just down the road. There seemed to be a never-ending line of people streaming out the doors.

"Hey, I wonder where they're going? It might be fun to follow them!" I suggested.

"You want to follow tourists? What about lunch?" Mom asked, glancing at her watch.

"It'll just be a few minutes. Come on, Mom. Where's your sense of adventure? We can get a free tour because I feel like I don't know this part of the city at all." So far, all of Mom's suggestions had been a bust, so it wasn't the worst idea to do what I wanted instead.

A tour guide holding a megaphone started talking.

"How's your Spanish?" Mom asked me after we listened to a few sentences.

"Muy bien," I answered.

Yes, I loved *Dora the Explorer* when I was a kid. So did you. Maps. Trying to find hidden objects. Going on adventures. It was a show that practically bred young pirates.

She almost smiled. "All right. I suppose this might do as a bit of enrichment."

We trailed behind the tour group as they walked. I strained to listen to the tour guide but realized I couldn't understand a thing, as my Spanish vocabulary from my *Dora*-watching days was sadly limited.

The large group slowly made their way down West Shipyard Street and, at Deacon Street, waited for the light.

"Come on," I urged. Walking at the back of the pack, we turned left onto Deacon Street and the neighborhood started to look different. The sidewalks were made of square cobblestones, and the area definitely had a different vibe than my neighborhood around Riverside.

"These sidewalks look really old," I said.

"I believe this was one of the first paved roads in Cedar Coast," Mom said.

Old stuff could be kind of cool. I could see why tourists would come here. It was the most unique part of the city.

The tour group was starting to spread out along the sidewalk like pulled taffy. We passed a souvenir shop and at the window, I slowed down to look. There was a T-shirt on display with a familiar face — Windy Willy! The image was less creepy than the wax figure from the museum had been. In the picture, he stood with one foot on the ground and one foot on top of a wooden barrel, his hands on his hips. Yup, definitely a pirate. It reminded me a lot of Brandon's new shirt.

"Come along." Mom dragged me away from the store window.

The people at the front had stopped walking, and the tour group was starting to form into a crowd at the end of the block. I heard the leader of a different tour group say in English, "The Rail's End steam clock is just ahead."

It was weird that so many tourists were coming to see the steam clock when I had never really even paid attention to it.

"Did you ever bring me to see the steam clock?" I asked Mom, who was trailing behind me.

"No, it's a tourist trap," she replied. She glanced at her watch again.

"But it's part of local history."

She snorted. "It was built in 1988."

"Oh," I replied, feeling a little silly. Of course, if it had been really important, Mom or Dad would have brought me here already. Maybe we should have just gone straight to the restaurant.

I heard a tour guide across the street say, "All right, folks, in just a few minutes, it's going to sound. This clock is something else! At noon, and *only* at noon, the Rail's End steam clock gives us a special treat. Twelve hoots of the whistle, all powered by a natural geothermal steam engine, the only one of its kind in the world! Followed by something special at the end. Let's hurry and claim our spots, before it gets too crowded."

"That sounds cool," I said, wondering what special thing a geothermal steam clock could possibly do. It certainly drew a crowd of people. It had to be somewhat interesting, didn't it? "Come on, we're here. May as well see what the big deal is." I pulled at Mom's sleeve.

"My feet are hurting — can we just go to the restaurant?" she asked, looking around.

"I want to see the noon whistle! You catch up!" My curiosity was piqued, and I wouldn't be hampered by a woman who wore tight shoes.

I heard Mom say my name, but I ignored her and rushed ahead. There were only a few minutes left before the whistle. All the other tourists started walking faster too.

The steam clock was about ten feet high. It looked like a really big, fancy grandfather clock. The body of the clock was mostly black, except you could see all the metal inner workings in the middle section, because it was encased in glass. It was very elaborate — this must have been the portion that harnessed the geothermal energy.

The top part was square and a bit larger than the body of the clock it was sitting on. Each side showed a clockface with roman numerals so you could see the time from every direction. At the very top was a triangular section acting like a roof, which had brass pipes sticking out of it. They almost looked like animal horns.

The inner workings, behind the glass, were spinning and whirling around. I got near the clock just as the first whistle started. The sound was nothing special. It was like a wimpy little train whistle, but with each whistle, a little burst of steam escaped from the pipes at the top and from a vent at the bottom, which I hadn't noticed before. Everybody around me had their cell phones out, taking videos. I managed to squeeze in between some people so that I was practically standing right in front of it.

Each of the next whistles was the same as the one before, and with each whistle, the cloud of steam grew larger. The mist started to collect and hover like a thick fog slowly enveloping the crowd from head to toe. I counted the whistles off in my head. *Eight, nine, ten . . .*

My arm started to tingle again. That was weird; it had felt fine since we left the museum. The steam cloud had grown even more now and was spreading out wider and thicker. Behind the glass section of the clock, parts were pumping up and down or spinning at high speed.

Eleven, twelve. A huge burst of steam escaped from the clock with an extra-loud, extra-long whistle that was like an unmuffled fart that wouldn't quit. The people around me laughed because it was so unexpected.

A tour guide said, "That's strange, I've never heard the whistle sound like that before."

In the middle of the long twelfth whistle, somebody behind me, who was jostling to get closer to the action, accidentally bumped me. Trying to keep my balance, I tumbled into the clock and ended up grabbing onto it to stop myself from falling.

When I touched its surface, both of my hands quivered and my body shuddered. The mist sent out by the steam clock rushed up toward my face as it completely shrouded me in a warm, dense fog. When the vapor dissipated and I let go, I wasn't standing next to the clock anymore.

CHAPTER 7

It was silent and I was alone. All the people who had been around me were gone. Nothing was familiar. No more fog. No more shops. No more steam clock. My eyes lifted upward to the small patch of sunlight that provided the only brightness in an otherwise dim space. It was like a halo of light about twenty feet above me, with a diameter of maybe ten feet. I had to blink hard and shake my head to convince myself that what I was seeing was real.

Right in the middle of the circle of light . . . was that the bottom of the steam clock? I craned my neck around and took a step back. The distinctive little pipes at the top of the clock — I could see them far above me. Somehow, I was *below* the clock, the sidewalk, and the road.

I stared up a little longer, trying to make sense of everything. The ring of light encircling the clock seemed blurrier toward the furthest outside edges and was clearest right in the middle, where the steam clock was. Beyond the circle of daylight, the ceiling above me took on a solid form — dark and dense, like the roof of a cave.

Through the shaft of light above, I could make out the shapes of people's feet as they walked by the clock. And then finally, I could hear something. The muted sound of traffic driving over the cobblestones up above made a *whomp, whomp* sound as tires sped quickly over the rough surface.

What the heck was this? I couldn't think straight. Where was I? The crowd of people that had been gathered around the steam clock began to move on, and when they did, they cleared the way for more light to filter down.

I looked around the area where I stood. I was surrounded by a wall of hard, packed dirt and loose stones, except on one side, about thirty feet from where I was standing, where there was a giant solid wall of rock at least twelve feet high, and even wider — maybe twenty feet across.

It felt like an underground pit. Since the only thing around me seemed to be dirt and rocks, I kept glancing straight up through the shaft of light. The light shifted and danced occasionally as people passed by the steam clock.

That was when I saw Mom. Even from underneath, I knew the distinctive sharp point of her shoe. She was standing right above me, perfectly still, in the spot where I had just been — had it only been a few seconds or was it a few minutes ago? I didn't know. My heart had already been pounding hard, but when I saw her, it raced.

Somehow, I found my voice and screamed, "Mom!"

For a fraction of a second, I thought she heard me. It was the way her head tilted to the side just a little bit. But when I saw her shoes walk away, it was all too much. I felt my knees go weak and I collapsed.

I was so groggy. My hearing kicked in before I could open my eyes.

"Is he all right?" a girl's voice asked.

"How should I know?" a man with a rough voice replied.

"You say you just found him here?" An older woman's voice this time. They all had distinctly British accents. I suddenly thought about Mom watching those movies based on old novels, where everybody wore very fancy clothes and sipped tea all the time.

"He appeared rather suddenly," the man said. "I was quite shocked when I first noticed him, so I did not approach him immediately. And then unexpectedly, he collapsed. I hadn't even the opportunity to introduce myself."

"Is he alive?" The girl's voice again, this time with a nervous edge.

"Young Abigail, I think he'd look quite different if he were dead!" The man laughed uproariously.

Looked like I wasn't dead — that was good news, I guess.

"Really, what an utterly inappropriate attempt at jocularity!" the woman said, clearly unimpressed.

Never before had I heard the word *jocularity* uttered in a sentence. Believe me, Mom uses words nobody else says all the time. *Mom.* She was probably getting help to find me right now. I hoped she wasn't getting too wrinkled worrying. I was fine, but she didn't know that.

"Mrs. Morris. After all these years together in the afterlife, I would have hoped you would have developed a sense of humor."

Afterlife? My head lolled to the side.

"Did you see that?" the young girl said. She must have been Abigail.

"Everybody, give him some space!" the woman, who I guessed was Mrs. Morris, spoke.

After what I assumed was everybody silently backing up, Mrs. Morris continued. "Young man! Can you hear me?" she yelled in my ear.

I winced.

"Definitely *not* dead!" Mrs. Morris proclaimed.

"This whole situation is making me very anxious," the girl named Abigail said. I imagined her putting down her cup of tea to wring her hands.

"Well, there's only ever been one live one down here before! Here is number two! Not exactly skilled in the art of resuscitating a fainting child, are we?" Mrs. Morris said.

One live one? Number two? What were they talking about? I wished I could open my eyes, but my lids refused to budge.

"Give the boy a moment. No good having you bellowing in his ear," the man's voice said.

"Very right, Mr. Sapperton," Mrs. Morris said.

Mr. Sapperton. The name seemed so familiar.

Now suddenly, my eyes popped open and somehow I sat up as best I could.

"Captain William J. Sapperton?" I asked, rubbing my eyes. My vision was blurry, and it was hard to focus.

"Why now, no need for such formalities. You may call me Mr. Sapperton if you like, but Willy will do."

I looked at the figures who stood before me, and my mind went blank. I was having what is commonly known as a "brain fart."

I closed my eyes and counted to three, hoping that when I opened them again, what I was seeing would somehow change.

Tentatively, I cracked one eye open. Nope, still the same! In front of me, these were not *people.*

Holy Jolly Roger! They were *ghosts.* My heart pounded forcefully in my chest.

Their figures were cloudy and indistinct. Shimmery and dull at the same time. There, and yet not there. I felt woozy and planted my hand down on the ground to brace myself. Ghosts! Talking ghosts! Talking to *me.*

Willy's ghost resembled the wax figure I had just seen earlier in the day. Something about him reminded me of looking at a TV without any cable reception, like jumping, jittery snowflakes across a screen. While it was hard to make out the details on his face, there was no ignoring his round belly, almost busting through the vest he wore under an overcoat.

Abigail wore a long-sleeved dress with a lace collar and lace at the cuffs. Her dark hair was tied in a braid down her back. She looked different from the captain. More like a soft, pillowy cloud, her features defined and clearer than Willy's. She looked to be about my age, maybe a year or two older, maybe a year or two younger. How could I know for sure? She was a ghost!

The woman had her hair in a style that looked like a puffed bun, and she wore a brooch at her neck. Her long, full skirt flowed wide around her ankles. Like the girl's, her form was definitely more solid than Willy's. Looking at her and Abigail was like looking at a faded black-and-white photograph.

All of them hovered in the air effortlessly, as if not touching the ground were the most natural thing in the world. Because, of course, they were *dead*.

"No, no, no. This cannot be happening. How did I even get here?" I muttered to myself, shaking my head.

"We were rather hoping you'd tell us the answer to that question," Mrs. Morris replied.

"I was just up there." I glanced up to the steam clock. "The noon whistle sounded, and now here I am."

"Oh, that old thing. It was very peaceful until they built it. Now once a day, it shakes and shivers down here. It's very annoying. Although I do like the light," Willy said.

"I just saw your wax statue!" I blurted out.

Everybody looked confused.

"Of Captain William J. Sapperton!"

"Please. Simply call me Willy."

"Right, right," I mumbled. "Sorry, *Willy*." I'd go by Captain if I were him, but maybe he was a pretty casual kind of guy. Wasted opportunity for people not to say, "Aye, aye, Captain!" if you asked me.

"Wax statue, you say?" he asked.

"Yeah, of you."

Willy smiled bashfully and looked quite pleased. As he smiled, his face became clearer and more focused. Now I could make out his thin mustache and trimmed beard, which I had not been able to see before. "A statue? Of me?" He held his left hand up to his chest. "Well, how unexpectedly wonderful." He paused briefly before he continued, "Was it to commemorate my achieve-ments in business or politics?"

"Uh, no," I answered. "You were part of a display."

"What kind of display?" he asked pleasantly.

"The title was 'Just a shipwrecked merchant captain or a PIRATE?' Pirate was in all caps."

I wanted to tell him how awesome it was that he was a pirate captain and that I was kind of honored to meet him, but I stopped myself because instead of looking pleased, he gave a deep sigh and turned away from me.

The young girl quickly moved her billowy figure in front of Willy and said, "My name's Abigail." She curt-sied. "This is my mother, Mrs. Emma Morris. We are pleased to make your acquaintance." She glanced back at Willy, who had folded his arms atop his stomach and was staring up at the shaft of light.

"Your name is . . . ?" Mrs. Morris questioned, leaning in, waiting for a reply.

My bandanna felt loose, so after I gave the knot a quick yank to tighten it, I took a deep breath before I replied, "My name is Stephen Oh-O'Driscoll." My voice quaked.

"Stephen Oh-O'Driscoll?" Willy turned to ask. "With a double *O*? *Oh*? *O'Driscoll*?" He spoke slowly and made my name into two questions, like everybody does. Then he added, "What kind of a name is that?" Willy looked like he was concentrating, trying to make sense of it. It was a lot like the face I had when I tried to do math without a calculator. I silently cursed my parents for my name — again.

Mrs. Morris and Abigail handled the news of my name more graciously.

"There are all sorts of names, aren't there? Some of them unique!" Abigail said kindly.

"Well, Stephen, we are very pleased that you have joined us in The Midway," Mrs. Morris said warmly.

"The Midway?" I asked.

Willy cleared his throat. "The Midway, as fine a home as any ghost could ask for!"

I caught Mrs. Morris and Abigail glancing at each other with eyebrows raised.

The place didn't feel *fine*. It felt like a tomb. "Is this *hell*?" I whispered, glancing around, half expecting boiling lava to explode through the floor at any time.

Willy chuckled. "Oh no, no, young Stephen. That's the *other* place. You've got to be a terribly lost cause to end up there."

Mrs. Morris and Abigail glanced at each other again.

"I like this one! This one is amusing," Willy said cheerfully. Then his mood darkened. "Not like that other young girl. When he first arrived, I thought it was finally her, had a bit of a thrill in the old bones, but alas, it was just him." Willy looked disappointed.

"Other young girl?" I asked. I felt like I was in a perpetual state of confusion.

"Willy," Mrs. Morris chastised. "You must know she's not coming back. It pains me to hear you even mention it again."

"A promise is a promise. And she promised she'd be back. That's the code — um, rather, that's the *principle* — that I live by." Willy seemed to set his jaw firm.

Code? I knew it! Willy lived by a *pirate code*! My heart fluttered. I didn't live by a pirate code, but I did have the Piventurate's Oath! Practically the same thing, with less theft and more fun! But he sure didn't seem thrilled about the display where he had been featured. I didn't get it at all.

"You know, we of all people understand," Mrs. Morris said gently as she gazed at Willy sympathetically.

He looked away.

"At any rate, Stephen, we welcome you most heartily and hope that you'll stay awhile," Mrs. Morris said graciously. For a dead soul, she seemed pretty nice.

"*Stay awhile?*" I mumbled.

"You still think you're running that inn of yours that burned you two to a crisp, eh?" Willy said.

My eyes were as big as baseballs.

"Hospitality is never out of fashion." Mrs. Morris lifted her chin high.

"What do you mean, *stay awhile?*" I asked again.

"This is The Midway. It is the first stage in the realm of the dead," Mrs. Morris said.

CHAPTER 8

Okay, okay. Just when things couldn't possibly be any weirder, she had to go and say "the realm of the dead." I swear, creepy music played in my head when she said it.

To try to calm myself, I reached into the back pocket of my track pants. I felt my Jolly Roger, and I was thankful I had had the good sense to covertly bring it with me today. No, it wasn't a *security blanket*, I'm not a baby; it was a *comfort item*. I needed comfort more than any twelve-year-old boy, *ever*.

"But *I'm* not dead. Am I?" I finally asked.

"We've established that you are indeed alive!" Mrs. Morris said cheerfully.

"Stephen," Abigail began.

I held up a finger. "Hang on. I think I need a minute." Standing seemed impossible, so I stayed seated.

You know when you're extremely stressed and people say stuff to you like "Just breathe"? Like you're not already obviously breathing, duh. My mind jumped to Brandon's mom trying to calm down in Mr. Huntington's office. She wasn't just trying to breathe; she was trying to find her center. Was "finding your center" a euphemism for *not* having an emotional breakdown? Whatever. I was feeling a bit desperate, so it was worth a go.

I closed my eyes and mouth but flared my nostrils as wide as they would go. With everything I had, I sucked in the stale air of The Midway and let it fill my lungs. My hands pushed the air, starting from my chest down to the top of my thighs.

"Whatever is he doing?" Mrs. Morris asked. I ignored her and the fact that I had three ghosts watching me sit and breathe.

I did it over and over. Okay, maybe three times.

Being calm when something like this was happening was harder than eating a side of boiled broccoli and carrots with no butter. But on the second deep breath, a new idea entered my head. Me, in the realm of the dead,

The Midway. Wasn't it also kind of incredible and awesome, like unlimited frozen yogurt with extra sprinkles?

Do *not* get me wrong, I was scared stiff, but I was trying hard to see the silver lining.

Brandon was never going to believe this. I dug my fingernails into my palm just to make sure this was all real. If it had been him instead of me, he'd probably be striding around here saying how cool it all was. I guess it *was* pretty cool — I was talking to *ghosts*. One of them might even be a ghost pirate captain.

Just before I opened my eyes, on the third breath, I reminded myself that as a piventurate, this was exactly the kind of event I should embrace. I said the Piventurate's Oath to remind myself that something like this was what I had always *thought* I wanted.

I had, of course, not anticipated being trapped inside the first stage of the realm of the dead, whatever *that* meant, but I guess that's what made it an adventure — the unexpected. So then why did I feel like puking?

Gurgle, growl, moan, rumble. I stared down at my stomach. Apparently, I could feel barfy and hungry at the same time. I had really been looking forward to my lunch special from Ye Olde Pasta Warehouse, but we hadn't made it there before all *this* happened. Still, I had more pressing concerns, like figuring out why the heck I was in the realm of the dead! There was no choice but to ignore my grumbling stomach.

"Any idea why I'm here?" I ventured. "You mentioned that there was another girl before?"

Mrs. Morris and Abigail looked at Willy, so I looked at him too.

He pretended to adjust his buttons.

"Mr. Sapperton? You were the only one to meet her, so you are best suited to answer his question," Mrs. Morris said.

This time, he leaned over and pretended to retie his shoelace.

Mrs. Morris straightened her back and said loudly, "Perhaps it's time you told us. The other one was here, and you say she left, but you've never told us exactly *how* she left. Only you know."

Willy looked away and stayed silent.

"Mr. Sapperton! There is a young boy, very much alive, who awaits your reply!" Mrs. Morris said forcefully.

He finally spoke. "I'm not telling tall tales! She *was* here. It's been quite a long time — I can't remember *everything*. I mostly remember her empty promises." Willy sighed. "She said she could help me. She told me she'd be back." His form flickered.

Mrs. Morris and Abigail gave each other *that look* again. I couldn't figure out what it meant.

"It's been so long," Willy said wistfully.

"How do I get back up there?" I pointed to the circle of light with the steam clock in the middle. "This is a cave or something, right? I can just walk out of here if I find the exit?" I asked hopefully, glancing around.

Abigail pressed her lips together, then spoke. "I'm afraid not. It's not like that at all."

"Please, Willy, anything else you can remember?" I begged.

Willy clasped his hands behind his back and floated back and forth. He appeared to be deep in thought. "I remember she wouldn't move away from the spot where the light comes in. At first, I thought she might be scared and needed it to feel safe. She stayed there, even when it turned dark." Willy looked up at the bottom of the steam clock. His face suddenly brightened. "Ah! She eventually fell asleep, but she slept restlessly.

She tossed and turned and started talking to herself. She said something like, 'When you lose your way, you need to go back to the beginning.' And then the next day, she was gone." Willy looked pleased. "That just came back to me. Maybe this ol' noggin still has some life!" He knocked on the side of his head.

Willy might have seemed happy with himself, but I sure wasn't feeling good about things. "But what does that even mean?" I cried.

"Sounds like a vexing riddle," Mrs. Morris said.

When you lose your way, you need to go back to the beginning. I never liked riddles to start — now I *hated* them with a burning passion. The beginning of what?

"So let's get real. I'm stuck here," I murmured, feeling dejected. "Willy, you don't really know how that girl left, do you?"

Willy looked indignant. "I've told you everything I can."

Everybody fell silent for a while. The reality of my situation was a downer. My brain was starting to spin a dazed loop.

Willy finally spoke. "Well, this has been a most eventful day. I'm ready for a rest. I'll be in my *private* spot." He gestured to a dark corner of The Midway, far away from the halo of light under the steam clock. He turned to leave.

"Fret not, Stephen. We'll figure something out for you," Mrs. Morris said gently. "I'll go ask the others. There must be a way for you to get home."

I nodded numbly. "Fret not" was right up there with "Just breathe." Mrs. Morris was already dead, what did *she* have to worry about? I was the one in trouble — stuck in an underground cave with no obvious way out and surrounded by ghosts.

Mrs. Morris said, "Abigail will keep you company. Perhaps you two can talk things over."

"Very well, Mother." Abigail nodded as Mrs. Morris started to float away. "I think it might be nice to put some distance between us and Willy," Abigail said to me, pointing to the side of The Midway that was dominated by the large wall of stone.

At the precise moment she pointed, Mrs. Morris flew right through the massive rock and disappeared.

CHAPTER 9

Not that a ghost flying through a huge solid wall of stone should have surprised me. But it *did*. She'd said she was off to see friends. I guess even the dead needed people to talk to. Speaking of the dead, The Midway seemed empty except for the four of us. There had to be more ghosts somewhere else.

I shook my head quickly. "Where did your mother go?" I asked Abigail. I got up and walked slowly in the direction she had just flown. This place didn't even give me time to wallow in my confusion.

"Go ahead, lass! Tell him. Tell him everything," Willy said with a raised voice from his dim corner. "Ol' Willy's a bit of a failure as a ghost, you see, young Stephen."

"I thought he wanted *me* to tell you," Abigail mumbled. "*Windy* Willy indeed."

I opened my mouth to ask a question, but the wind in Windy Willy kept going.

"I'm trapped in The Midway. We're not supposed to stay here. It's only supposed to be the first step! We're supposed to go and be *free*. But lo and behold, ol' Willy's the only ghost trapped here. Everybody else can come and go as free as the spirit of a bird. Not me. I'm trapped in this . . . cage." He sighed deeply. "Oh, and don't think you two have me duped. You Morrises just come to check on me. It's kind of you but makes me feel like a fool. Gah!" Willy huffed.

I glanced over at Abigail. She simply shrugged.

"How can a ghost be trapped?" I asked.

"Do you not suppose I've asked myself that very same question a thousand times?" Willy flew a bit closer to us and threw his hands up in the air. "I cannot fly through that foul rock!" He glared over at the large wall Mrs. Morris had so easily passed right through only minutes before.

"Mr. Sapperton!" Abigail spoke with authority, and Willy seemed to cower at her words. "That is quite enough. You asked me to tell Stephen, so *I* will tell him. Take a rest, sir!"

"You Morrises are quite bossy," Willy replied crossly.

Out of the corner of my eye, I caught some movement. A few other ghosts were tentatively sticking their faces through the rock before bashfully disappearing too quickly for me to get a really good look at them. This was getting freakier by the minute.

"Seems the spirit folk are starting to talk already," Abigail said, pointing to them, but they had disappeared as suddenly as they had arrived. "Mother *does* like to share stories."

"Who are they?" I shouldn't have been surprised to see more ghosts, because the whole "realm of the dead" thing implied dead people, lots of dead people, but I was anyway.

"Local spirits, like me. People tend to stay close to home."

My eyeballs felt dry because I wasn't sure I had blinked recently.

"Stephen," Abigail said in a hushed voice. "There is much to tell you. I hardly know where to begin!"

I swallowed hard. "I'll start. What's on the other side?" I jerked my head toward the big wall of rock.

Abigail took a deep breath. "*The Great Sea is the place where we are free.*" It was as though she'd sung the phrase, and the air in The Midway shimmered briefly. My skin prickled as her words hung in the air.

"The Great Sea," I repeated slowly. When I said it, my words did not sing, but I felt something quiver in the air around me.

"That's where spirits really belong," Abigail said.

"I wouldn't know!" Willy shouted. The form of his spirit flickered, like a malfunctioning LED bulb.

"Please, Mr. Sapperton," Abigail begged, floating closer to him and his dim corner. "You've been quite a marvelous host to our visitor. But it is time to rest. Please rest."

"All right, lass," he said with little vigor. He complied and returned to his corner. Like an obliging kindergartner, he lay down in his spot.

I kept my voice as low as possible. "Let me get this straight. Willy is the only ghost who is stuck in The Midway?" I asked, my mind turning. I had no idea that death was a multistaged event. Wasn't dead just *dead*?

"Yes, it is most curious, isn't it?"

"Nobody knows why?" I asked. Willy's problems almost made me temporarily forget about my own. *Almost*.

"It is a great mystery," Abigail said.

"What's so great about the next stage compared to here?" I pointed in the general direction her mother had disappeared.

Silently, she shushed me as I must have raised my voice.

"Oh, this is rather a . . . how shall I put it?" Abigail glanced around The Midway. "A place where the spirits wait."

Waiting was the worst. Ever waited for a doctor's appointment that was scheduled for two o'clock but then at, say, two thirty they call your name, and you jump up and think, *Finally! My turn!* But you just get ushered into an exam room and then you wait *again*. When the doctor finally strides in, you're so grateful to be seen, even if it's now three o'clock, all that angry impatience you had bottled up inside you just kind of disappears. I wondered if this was Willy's predicament — being stuck in the exam room, waiting for your turn.

We fell silent for a while, and I stood with the mammoth stone in front of me. It was one giant slab. I had to crane my neck to look up to the top. No fissures, no cracks. Carefully, I reached out to touch it. There was a faint coarseness to the surface, and it was surprisingly warm. A gentle heat radiated off its surface and my hands felt soothed. But not just my hands. My stomach had been in knots the whole time I was down here, and now I suddenly felt okay. Calm, almost.

There must have been something extraordinary behind and beyond this rock. Something that Willy could not see or be a part of. Part of me wished I could see The Great Sea for myself.

"This rock is The Nexus," Abigail told me quietly. "The separation between waiting and a soul's freedom."

"What do spirits wait for?" I whispered. "Why don't they just go straight through?"

"It's different for each person," she replied, her words barely audible. "Some do go straight through. Most are ready, but there are some that wait for a loved one. Some wait for themselves to feel ready. This place is important for those who need it, but in Willy's case . . ." She seemed unable to finish her thought.

"But Willy can't move on? He's tried everything?"

"Everything." She paused for a moment. "Something is holding him back. Like a chain tied around his waist that he cannot accept or acknowledge."

"What could it be?" I murmured. The small of my back felt almost hot from leaning against the rock that was trapping Willy. What was he *really* waiting for? I turned and sat down against the stone wall.

She furtively peeked in his direction. "Nobody knows. Especially not Willy. But that's not quite the whole story."

Abigail leaned in very close as if she needed to whisper something into my ear. Her hand brushed my left shoulder as she started to say something — I *felt* it — but she didn't get to finish her sentence. Because that was when I fell backwards through the rock wall into The Great Sea.

CHAPTER 10

I had almost started to get used to the dim light of The Midway when I suddenly found myself lying on a pebbly beach squinting up at a blue sky. It was much brighter than The Midway, but the sky above still looked hazy, like a foggy day. Yet somehow, despite the fog, the air still shimmered.

I propped myself up. Instead of sitting with my back *against* The Nexus, I was now sitting *facing* it. Around the huge stone, the beach formed a horseshoe shape, and it was ringed with thick, scrubby bushes. I ventured a look over my shoulder. Behind me, water lapped at the shore. There was a vast open expanse of water to one side, and to the other, a small inlet ringed with low green hills.

The spirits were everywhere off in the distance. It was almost like they were dancing across the surface of the water, and as their spirits floated above it, the water sparkled underneath them.

The air hummed gently and a feeling of calm came over me. I breathed deeply and closed my eyes. Now I understood why when Abigail had said, *The Great Sea is the place where we are free*, it sounded like a beautiful song. This place felt calm and joyful, almost as though I could touch the happiness with the tips of my fingers. It seemed like a pretty decent hang-out for eternity.

Despite being in such a beautiful and peaceful setting for ghosts, I found that my head, still attached to my very alive body, ached. I felt like I had just been punched. Then again, I *had* just passed through a wall of solid rock. Not only did I have a throbbing in my temples but my left shoulder felt prickly, like when you sit cross-legged for too long and your feet have fallen asleep. I gave it a good scratch to get rid of the uncomfortable feeling before I rubbed my forehead and tried to think, but that was proving impossible.

"Stephen?" Abigail shouted frantically. Her face was sticking out of the large wall of rock, right in the middle of it.

I looked up and our eyes met. "Hey," I said.

"How can this be?" she exclaimed, her eyes big and bulgy like Mom's.

I shrugged my shoulders in a very exaggerated way. How did I know what was going on? First time visitor, remember?

Before I could say anything, the most monstrous noise echoed across the harbor. Something like the sound a cat makes when it unexpectedly meets a skunk in the middle of the night, but louder and much more irritating. It was a sharp, piercing cry that made the hairs on the back of my neck stand at attention. I held my hands up to my ears to block the noise, but it soon stopped.

Abigail's mouth popped open wide enough to fit a grapefruit inside.

"Wait!" Abigail said to me. She disappeared back through the rock.

As if I had a choice.

The horrific noise was back. But louder and more intense. My shoulder wasn't the only part of me that felt weird anymore — my entire body buzzed. I covered my ears again.

The feeling of joy that had once surrounded The Great Sea instantly disappeared. Abigail did not mention that this place was so noisy. The view was nice and all that, but it was *loud*.

Because I had my ears covered, and because I was wincing, I didn't notice them right away. All the ghosts had stopped gliding and moving in the distance. Instead, they were now hovering near me at the water's edge, so close I could see all their faces.

This cluster of spirits was shimmery and quite well-defined. All sorts of different-looking people. Some very old (you could tell by their clothes, which looked similar to the Morrises'), and some newer (like one spirit wearing ripped jeans and a baggy hoodie).

I felt their eyes on me, and there was a kind of aggressive heat from their stares. I trembled.

Mrs. Morris pushed her way to the front of the gathering crowd. I was thankful for her friendly face.

"Stephen?" She looked stunned. "What are *you* doing here?"

"Surprise?" I faked a tense smile.

Abigail came rushing back through the rock and skidded to a halt next to me.

Mrs. Morris looked at her daughter. "Is it what we fear it might be?"

The ghosts around Mrs. Morris started to mutter to themselves.

Abigail nodded affirmatively.

Mrs. Morris turned to face the gathering ghosts. "This is much more serious than we thought. We all knew his time was coming to an end. But now, maybe he knows it too. Let's give him comfort as best we can. I'm not sure there is much else we can do."

Another colossal howl. Involuntarily, my body turned to face the direction of the noise. The rock. Did the noise come from behind The Nexus? Was that sound made by *Willy*?

"Abigail, keep Stephen company," Mrs. Morris ordered. "This boy is full of surprises."

"Yes, Mother."

Mrs. Morris dashed forward and, with a wave of her arm, motioned for everybody to join her. In a surprisingly orderly way, all the ghosts who had assembled approached The Nexus. As one large mass, they disappeared through it. All except for one soul, who lingered behind and stared at me a little too long.

"Look away," Abigail said to me hurriedly. But it was too late. I had already met his gaze. What a mistake.

"What have you got here, eh, missy?" This spirit seemed old and rough. He wore a tattered brimmed hat and an overcoat that looked to have been patched and repaired. A frayed rope was tied around the waist instead of a belt. On his face, I could see the remains of a scar down the side of his cheek — a scar that hadn't quite healed, so it looked like he had been sliced open. Just the sight of him gave me cold, petrified chills.

"A live one, eh?" he asked Abigail with a voice that made my skin crawl. "Well, that's a first." His creepy eyes tracked up and down my body. "Must be something more to you for you to be here." Then he looked directly at me.

I tried to swallow but my throat felt stuck.

"You don't look all that impressive, though, eh? What's your story, lad?" he hissed as he came closer.

"None of your business!" Abigail spoke firmly.

I bowed my head a little and let Abigail do all the talking.

He cackled ominously. "Full of courage and vinegar today, aren't we, lass? But this one here . . ." He looked at me again. Why did he keep looking at me? "You've not got much to say, do you, boy?" I felt what I thought was his breath dance across my face.

I was going to need a fresh pair of underwear.

"I'll go ask my ol' captain, then." He tilted his head in the direction of the massive rock.

Hold up. Willy had been this creepy guy's *captain*?

"Please make yourself useful!" Abigail said forcefully. "It's the least you could do!"

"Oh, I'm not done quite yet. It's not over until it's over." He whipped past me, and I felt my shirt flutter before he vanished through The Nexus.

"Foul man," Abigail said, disgusted.

Maybe all ghosts weren't as friendly as Abigail and her mother.

"Who was *that*?" I asked, trying to hide my trembling voice. "And what is going on?"

"Never mind him. He's nasty."

"He said Willy was his captain."

"Yes, a long time ago." Abigail nodded. "I do believe Willy has tried to distance himself from some of his acquaintances. They are rather rough characters, aren't they?"

The howling started up again. I grimaced in agony. It would have been more pleasant to listen to a car alarm blaring all night, accompanied by an eager novice violin player, than to listen to *that* sound.

"Is that noise coming from Willy?" I yelled loudly.

"Yes, I'm afraid so," Abigail replied with her voice raised.

"Why?" I yelled.

The noise stopped temporarily.

"Oh dear." Abigail wrung her hands. She looked away.

"Tell me. What's going on?" I pressed.

She let out a puff of air. In the light of The Great Sea, she looked luminous. Even in The Midway, I could tell that she was more stable than Willy, but with the light here, she looked different again. Still dead, yet *almost* lively.

"The noise Willy makes is called Transcendent Affliction. I'd heard stories about it, but that was the first time I'd heard it myself." Abigail sighed deeply. "It's a sign that he's . . ." Her lips shut tight.

"Please tell me," I urged.

"He's given up hope." Abigail's shoulders slouched.

"Why?"

She would not look me in the eye.

"Come on, please?"

"Because of you," she said carefully.

"Me?" I exclaimed. "What did *I* do?"

She gestured with her arms open wide to The Great Sea.

"Oh." I guess he'd been trying to get here for basically his entire afterlife, and I just fell backward into it, butt-first.

"A spirit who has given up hope, well, without it, how can one enter this final, glorious realm? There's more. The part I didn't tell you yet," she hinted. She hunched over like she was telling me a secret she shouldn't be revealing.

I eagerly leaned in, my heart pounding vigorously.

"His time is almost up," Abigail whispered.

"He's already dead," I said, confused.

"There is a truth spoken by those who know. It comes from The Vast Sea."

"Where's that?"

"Far from here, where the spirits are ancient and many lifetimes of experience have been passed down," Abigail told me. "Not like the souls around this place. The ghosts here are a lot younger. We're not knowledgeable about these things."

I listened carefully.

"There is a natural order to death. We leave the earthly world and visit The Midway. Once we are ready, we come here." Abigail looked behind her. "As you can see, The Great Sea is quite wondrous."

I nodded in agreement.

"However, if a spirit does not pass after a hundred years, there is some . . . difficulty. Spirits that stay in The Midway for too long, well, their souls are . . ." She let out a sharp cry and covered her mouth. "It's almost too much to bear!"

"What? What happens?"

Abigail gathered her thoughts. "Souls that linger too long, they've disrupted the natural order. One's journey in the afterlife should be a rather straight line, from The Midway to The Great Sea. But there is a less-traveled path, a cruel fork in the road, so to speak. After a hundred years, those unfortunate souls are lost and can never find their way back to the ultimate freedom that The Great Sea affords."

"Never?" I asked.

"Never," Abigail said decisively.

"Like, really no hope whatsoever?" I persisted.

"They are cursed to go . . . *to the other place.*" She pointed her finger down to the ground.

"*Hell?*"

She sighed. "I suppose that when I was alive, I had the image of a fiery pit in the bowels of the earth too."

I tried to suppress it, but an inappropriate chuckle escaped, because you can't say "fiery pit" and "bowels" in the same sentence without making me laugh. "Sorry," I said quickly, knowing this was no laughing matter.

Abigail gave me a confused look but continued. "But now that I'm here, I know that there is no burning pit in the center of the world."

That wasn't *technically* right. Hadn't she ever seen a cross-section of the earth?

"It's The Chasm. Usually, it's reserved for the most vile souls that ever lived. Those without a single shred of human decency. But it's not just for the truly evil. It's also for those who are . . ." She let out a muffled gasp again. "Oh, poor Mr. Sapperton! I hadn't even *thought* of that part. He'll be surrounded by the worst sorts down there."

"Worse than that guy?" I motioned with my finger and drew a line down my cheek.

"Much worse."

"Does Willy know this?"

"No, no. We've kept it from him. All of the local spirits have made a pact. We think it's better that he not know. And I suppose that, in a way, we always hoped that something could be done to help him," she said. "Mother and I check up on him periodically. To make sure . . ."

"That's he's still there?" I finished her sentence. I felt myself go pale.

"Surely you noticed that he looks different than the rest of us?" she asked. "That's been happening for quite some time."

"Yes, I noticed."

"He's not got long. Perhaps even less time than we imagined with the onset of Transcendent Affliction."

I stared down at the pebbles on the beach and closed my eyes. The breeze danced across the skin on my face, and the ends of my bandanna tickled my neck. Willy's afterlife was the saddest ghost story I had ever heard.

There had been no more hideous screaming for a while, and it was quiet. A few of the ghosts started to make their way back through the rock. I would have been completely oblivious if I hadn't noticed their lingering glares in my direction. Not just casual stares either, but eyes that blamed me and practically seared my skin.

It wasn't my fault that Willy was going to go to The Chasm, but it sure was my fault that he had to suffer from Transcendent Affliction before he made his way there.

CHAPTER 11

Staring out at the water of The Great Sea was strangely calming, and my headache finally disappeared. I found myself taking my own personal Mindful Minute. When I opened my eyes, the sun was sitting just above the horizon. I didn't know if time in The Great Sea matched the time in Cedar Coast, because my watch flashed uselessly down here, but it seemed like late afternoon already! Time seemed slippery. A few more ghosts had passed through the large wall of stone, but there was still no sign of Mrs. Morris.

Abigail and I sat quietly together for some time, and I was finally starting to process the day, but after sitting on a pebbly beach for too long, I needed to stretch my legs. Piventurates explore, I reminded myself. I needed to get up and investigate the beach.

The bushes that flanked both sides of The Nexus were thorny and formed an impenetrable wall. I could not see above the dense foliage, so I tried to peer through gaps in the branches.

Something white caught my eye in amongst the jagged dark-green leaves. I pulled the sleeve of my shirt down to protect my skin from the thorns, which were real enough, so that I could reach through the tangled mess. If there was one thing I was good at, it was picking through foliage.

The branches made me think of Brandon. What had he done during today's lunch hour without me? It was hard to practice sword fighting alone. Somehow I thought he'd have tried anyway.

I could see the object better now — it looked like a piece of painted, hand-planed wood, but it was hard to tell. I gave it a hard tug and fell on my butt. The Crocs gave me no traction whatsoever on the pebbly beach. I got over any feeling of embarrassment quickly because emerging through the tangled mess of thorns, leaves, and branches was the prow of a small boat! My face lit up.

"Whatever are you doing over here?" Abigail floated closer. I picked myself up hurriedly and wiped the back of my pants with my hands.

"You've dropped something." She pointed to the ground.

My Jolly Roger had fallen out of my pocket. I reached over to quickly pick it up, suddenly self-conscious about it.

Abigail watched me shove it roughly back into my pocket.

"Is that a . . ." She paused. "No, no, it couldn't be."

"What do you think it is?" I asked haltingly.

"A Jolly Roger?" she guessed.

"How do you know what a Jolly Roger is?" I was shocked. The little boat I had just found seemed unimportant now.

She smiled slightly. "My gramps." She raised her eyebrows. "Mother doesn't like me to talk about it. It's not polite conversation, she says."

My pulse raced. "I think I understand. But you can tell me more."

"He brought me a coconut once," she whispered. "From his travels. But Gramps and Gran did not have a good relationship. They lived apart and Gran had a hard life. Mother blamed Gramps and his *lifestyle* for it."

"My parents live apart too."

"He loved being out on the water. Exploring. He couldn't help himself — it called to him." She looked over at the water of The Great Sea. It twinkled in the light and her eyes glowed. "But Mother holds a bit of a grudge and has kept me away from him."

I knew I needed to tell her. If there was anybody who was going to understand, it would be her.

"I'd like to be a *piventurate* one day." I said the word as slowly and as clearly as I could. My heart pounded fiercely in my chest. "Do you know what that means?"

"Piventurate." She said it carefully. After a moment, the corners of her mouth turned up. "That would be somebody like Gramps. Not really a nasty pirate type — oh, there are plenty of those. But there is another kind of sailor, isn't there? A person with an insatiable yearning to see what else the world has to offer."

Now *that* was a good definition.

From the moment I had met her, I knew I liked her. Now I understood why.

"So, you totally get it," I said, nodding with approval.

"Totally," she replied.

The way she'd spoken was so out of character for her, I started laughing. She laughed with me.

"So, I was wondering if you could explain something," I asked Abigail when the laughter subsided. All this talk about her gramps and his piventurate ways reminded me of Mr. Sapperton. "What's the deal with Willy? Why doesn't he want to be called 'Captain'?" What could have been better?

"That's rather a good question," Abigail said softly.

Just then, Mrs. Morris finally appeared. She was one of the last ghosts to leave The Midway.

"*Shh.*" Abigail glanced sideways at me furtively. Our conversation about piventurates was over. "Mother!" Abigail perked up. "Tell me."

Mrs. Morris reached out to stroke her daughter's cheek. "It's as bad as it can be, my dear. We've managed to calm him, but that silly old ninny Mrs. Beaufois brought her looking glass and Willy caught sight of himself in it."

"Ghosts can hold onto things?" I asked. My hand suddenly reached for my left shoulder, and I remembered how it had felt when Abigail brushed against it.

"Yes, it must be something we most urgently need and desperately want. Most of us have decided to let everything go, but there are a few who have convinced themselves that they need some kind of reminder of their past, like that vain goat, Mrs. Beaufois. Beau*fool* is what she is! I'm just so furious with her!" Mrs. Morris grumbled. "She practically held it up in front of his face as she was checking her hairstyle. Oh, pride will be the downfall of many!"

"How did he take it, when he saw himself?" Abigail asked.

"He just lay down on the ground, all calm-like. He's not moved since." Mrs. Morris pressed her lips together. "It was almost better when he was howling. At least then he had some energy left in him."

The three of us stood around feeling dejected and sad for Willy. He wasn't exactly *nice* — probably the third-nicest ghost I had met in The Midway and The Great Sea — but he was definitely better than the scary-looking dude.

Mrs. Morris looked up at me, and then looked past me into the bushes.

"What is that?" she asked.

Abigail perked up and peered in the same direction as her mother.

Because of all that talking about pirates and piventurates, I had almost forgotten about the boat.

"It's a . . ." I started to say. But my words failed me.

"A dory!" Abigail exclaimed.

I smacked my head. It wasn't like I was a boat *expert* or anything, but I had read my fair share of books on boats, and it seemed that I should have remembered the humblest vessel of them all. Clearly, my brain wasn't working right.

"A dory," I repeated. I pushed up my sleeves.

"What's it doing here?" Mrs. Morris asked. "That's most strange."

Her eyes shifted from me back to the dory, and then rapidly back in my direction. She straightened her back and took a deep breath.

"Never mind the dory. We've got another problem." Mrs. Morris flicked her chin at me.

"What is it?" I asked.

"My dear boy, look at your arm."

Abigail covered her mouth and gasped.

That's because I was fading away.

CHAPTER 12

Down here, I was talking to myself a lot. After noticing that my forearm was less solid than it should have been, I found it was easy to jump to the conclusion that I was *disappearing* into thin ghost-air. I said a bunch of other things to myself:

Be chill, Stephen, you're not dead yet.

Dead people aren't hungry, and you're definitely hungry.

Piventurates don't freak out with just a little disappearing. Freak out when you're all gone.

I lifted my shirt to look at my stomach. Same as my arm. I was taking on the haziness of The Great Sea.

"Mother, you are very connected to the stories of the collective spirits. You must know what to do." Abigail looked at her mother confidently.

Mrs. Morris appeared unsure. "This is unprecedented territory." She spoke slowly. "My dear, while I am quite knowledgeable about the stories of old, in this case, I'm afraid I don't know what to do. There has never been a live one in The Great Sea to tell stories about."

The feeling of panic probably should have come to me before this moment, but for some reason being in The Great Sea had taken away any anxiety. I had felt reasonably good. No fits of crying. No fits of rage. I had just taken it all in. Not that anything made sense, but I was handling it like a champ. But I guess the straw that broke my back was disappearing body parts — *my* disappearing body parts. This place sure was pretty, but it was for *them*, not for me. Not even The Great Sea could temper the feeling of dread that started to slowly suffocate me.

"I have to get out of here." I spoke calmly. But I didn't *feel* calm. "Not just The Great Sea, The Midway too. I have to get home."

Abigail started flitting around like a nervous mouse and just kept saying, "Oh dear, oh dear."

She wasn't helping at all.

My legs needed to *move*. I walked right up to the rock and stared it down. How *had* I passed through it?

I put my hands up against it and pushed as hard as I could. Its warmth enveloped my hands, but it didn't budge. No wonder Willy hated this thing so much! Why couldn't it have been a doorway?

I stopped pushing and stood in front of the rock, wishing I had laser-beam eyes. The skin on my palms felt weird, like the time I had chopped jalapeño peppers with my bare hands — strangely warm, with a fiery but gentle spark. I stared at my hands while I opened and closed my fists.

"It seems I need to go travel a bit farther and talk to the others. Learn anything I can," Mrs. Morris said.

I dropped my hands to my sides and my right hand reached into my pocket. I gave my Jolly Roger a squeeze.

"You're leaving again?" I tried to keep down the low-key panic in my voice.

"I'm no use to you here," Mrs. Morris said, before turning to her daughter and glancing at The Nexus. "If he starts up again, I'll be back."

"Come back as quickly as you can," Abigail said.

"Now, now." Mrs. Morris made a motion as if she were chucking me under my chin. I must have looked really pathetic. "I know it seems like a rather hopeless situation. But I think you've forgotten something."

I peeled my eyes up off the rocky beach to look at her. "What's that?"

"You are the first live one to ever see The Great Sea," Mrs. Morris reminded me. "You must believe that it is for a reason." Mrs. Morris twirled around and in the blink of an eye, she was dashing across the water and was soon beyond my sight.

I let her words sink in and tried to stand up straighter.

You know what? Getting cheered up by a ghost wasn't half bad. I decided she was right. I *must* be here for a reason. I just didn't know what it was yet.

The Great Sea had gone calm — too calm. Not a spirit in sight except for Abigail, who was floating up and down the edge of the shore, almost as if she were pacing. The only sound was the water lapping at the edge of the beach.

My hand was still clenching my Jolly Roger, but as I walked by The Nexus, I caught sight of the dory, which I hadn't quite finished pulling out of the bushes.

I scampered up to the small boat and pulled it further out. An absurd idea came to me. I made sure Abigail wasn't looking, then I jammed my flag into a crack on the prow and stood back to take a look.

I half laughed, half despaired at what I saw. It hung limply, almost as if it was stuck in by accident. Not exactly the image I had had in mind of my flag flapping majestically in the wind.

I gave my head a shake before snatching the flag out of the crack and shoving it back in my pocket before Abigail could see. My priorities were all wrong. Flying my Jolly Roger on a broken-down little dory should have been low on my list — like, barely even top ten. Priority number one: Get out of here!

I took a peek under the sleeve of my shirt. Still less solid than I should be, but no worse than a few minutes ago. Time for a reset. Back to the rock.

I wandered back over to The Nexus and leaned on it, wondering what the heck to do. After a few seconds, the skin on my back felt tingly, almost electric, just like my hands had felt earlier. I pulled away from it.

"Is something the matter?" Abigail asked. She stopped pacing and flew closer to me.

"I felt something. Oh, I was probably just imagining it, never mind."

My back turned to the rock again, I slid down to the ground and used it like a back rest.

"Abigail?"

"Hmm?"

"How am I going to get out of here?" I whispered. "I don't belong in the realm of the dead." A feeling of dread was creeping into the pit of my stomach. I threw my head back against the rock and closed my eyes. My bandanna slid askew, and I didn't even care.

"Your head-covering has come loose," Abigail said.

I pried my eyes open just enough to see her reaching over to help adjust my bandanna. When she touched my head, I fell backwards into The Midway.

CHAPTER 13

I landed with a thud — my butt firmly and painfully hitting the ground. I'd fallen butt-first into The Great Sea and that was how I returned from it. Wasn't I classy?

Next time, if there *was* a next time, I was going to try walking in with some dignity. My backside was really starting to ache.

Moments later, Abigail flew in and hovered over me.

"Well, that was interesting." She gave her hands a long look and then stared at where she had touched my head.

The tingles on my scalp felt like little sparks. I gave myself a good scratch. We stared at each other for several moments and then it clicked. Abigail. *She'd* made it possible. She'd brushed my shoulder — *boom*, I was in

The Great Sea. She'd touched my head — *boom*, I was back in The Midway.

"It's you," I whispered to her.

"Me?" Her eyes opened wide.

Then we heard a little whimper.

Just as Mrs. Morris had reported, Willy was lying down motionless, with his arm draped across his face. Nearby was the only shaft of light. His form was barely visible at all. He looked like a pencil sketch that was almost completely rubbed away. Just a faint outline remained. He was close to finally disappearing.

Willy turned away from us, but he spoke. "Why you? Why *you*? How?" His voice was shaky.

"I'm sorry," I said. The guilt was eating me up.

"No matter," he said softly. "It's almost done."

Abigail quietly brought her fist up to her mouth and tried to suppress a sob. She couldn't look at Willy anymore and kept her eyes firmly on the ground. The funeral vibes she was giving off were downright gloomy! He'd already died once, and it didn't seem fair that he was going to have to do it all over again.

"It's not over!" I said to her. "Not yet! He's still here." I tried to keep my voice down. Nobody likes it when people talk about them like they're not there.

"There's nothing wrong with my hearing, boy," Willy said without moving.

"Then hear this — there is always hope! I'm stuck in the realm of the dead and I haven't given up yet. Neither should you. There has to be something you can do. Something you've never tried before."

Willy grunted and then said faintly, "I saw myself. In the looking glass." There was a sereneness to his voice that I didn't like. It was the way somebody speaks when they've given up completely.

"Mrs. Beaufois!" Abigail muttered angrily under her breath.

"Lass, it was time I knew. I do thank you for trying to spare my feelings all these years."

"Mr. Sapperton. There is always hope," I told him again.

He curled up into a soft ball and said, "Hope is only for the living."

The light from above was very thin, occasionally punctuated by quick bright flashes. I could only assume it was the headlights of passing cars. I was tired. Really, really tired.

Unlike Willy, I still had hope that Mrs. Morris would come back with some newfound knowledge about how I could make my final escape from The Midway. Abigail kept glancing over at the wall of stone.

"Do you want to go?" I asked her.

"I *would* like to find my mother," she confessed.

"No problem. You go ahead. I should probably get some sleep anyway." I suppressed a yawn.

"You'll be all right?"

I nodded. "I don't think I'm going anywhere. Just come back tomorrow." I stole a glance at my arm. It was hard to see with the dim light, but I didn't look much fuzzier than I had in The Great Sea. Maybe I'd even be alive tomorrow.

"I shall," she agreed. "We'll figure this out. I'm sure my mother has talked to everybody by now. She must have learned *something*."

She slowly made her way toward The Nexus before she took a final glance over her shoulder. I gave her a wave. "I'll be okay. Thanks for staying with me this whole time. We had a bit of an adventure, didn't we?"

She winked. "Just as proper piventurates should." Before I knew it, she was gone.

"What on earth is a piventurate?" Willy asked weakly after Abigail had disappeared.

He'd been so quiet that I'd kind of forgotten about him for a minute.

Now with Abigail gone, I wondered if maybe I could talk to Willy privately — one-to-one, pirate-to-piventurate. Sometimes it was easier to talk to a stranger than to somebody who really knew you, wasn't it? Mom had talked to a woman named Carol once a week for a long time after she split up with Dad. I talked to Carol too, for a while. When you talk to somebody you don't know, they don't judge you the same way as somebody close to you might.

Would the captain feel better talking? He couldn't feel *worse*, could he?

"It's a new way of thinking about pirates," I told him.

He snorted and looked away.

"So, there's something I've been meaning to ask." I tried to keep casual. "Were you?"

"Was I what?"

"You know." I raised my eyebrows slightly. "A pirate captain. You might say I'm like-minded."

His eyes moved from the Crocs I was wearing on my feet slowly up my body until they stopped at the top of my head, and he gave my bandanna a long, lingering stare. "Now, I don't know what a lad like you thinks he knows about pirates, but here's what I know: You must be a rugged and tough sort. Life on a ship is full of adversities. Dressing the part of a pirate with a silly little scarf does not mean one *is* a pirate or has the right stuff to become one."

Now, talking might have made Willy feel better, but it wasn't helping *me* at all. My face felt hot and prickly. I knew I never wanted to be a pirate in a traditional sense — this is why the world so desperately needs the word *piventurate*! Why wouldn't anybody from Dictionary. com reply to the online request form that Brandon and I had filled out together? What was the point of having a feedback form if you were never going to accept any new words?

Trying to have a serious talk with Willy was a choice I was beginning to regret. In fact, it was now my deepest wish for him to shut up and leave me alone, but the wind in Willy kept going. "I like you, lad."

This was how he talked to people he *liked*? Remind me not to get on his bad side.

"You amuse me. Not like the other one," he said.

The other one. Right. The one who had managed to get out of here. Just knowing that somebody else had left at least gave me hope that I could too. I mean, I might have been stuck here slowly disappearing, but I also had to believe that I might be able to go home too. If only Willy could just give me some more specific details!

I worked hard to shake off what he had said about me, my Crocs, my bandanna, and oh, basically everything that was important to me. I really just wanted to curl up and go to sleep, but I needed more information.

"Mr. Sapperton?" I ventured, swallowing any remaining pride I had. "About how the other one left. Do you think it makes sense if . . ."

He cut me off and said, "I've already told you everything I remember. She was here, and then she was gone." His tone had become irritable and as he spoke, his shadowy figure flashed in and out.

Now I knew why Carol charged so much money. Getting somebody to talk about their feelings was hard work, and then sometimes they said things that were mean.

"I do believe it's time for us to rest," Willy said. "You must be tired."

Mom sometimes said this kind of thing instead of "Go away." Obvious hint received.

"Good night, young Stephen," he said, floating right up close to me.

The corners of his eyes crinkled, and his mouth tightened. He gave the lapels of his jacket a final tug before he floated away to a dark corner of The Midway. He was as faint as I had ever seen him. It wouldn't be long now, even I could see that.

"Good night, Willy."

For just a moment, I felt relieved that he didn't want to keep talking. He didn't have any more information that would help me anyway. But then my heart skipped a beat. What if he was gone when I woke up?

I didn't want it all to end this way. I wanted to say things. But everything I thought about saying seemed so useless. "You'll be okay" was a lie. He wasn't okay. He was going to be cast off into The Chasm soon.

It reminded me of all the times people at school or relatives used to try to cheer me up when they heard that Mom and Dad were splitting up. It didn't take me long to figure out that they weren't saying things to make *me* feel better — they were saying things to make *themselves* feel better.

I didn't need to say anything to him. But I wondered if there was something I could *do*. There had to be something. I didn't want to rub it in his face, but I *had* just gone and seen The Great Sea. He'd been trying for almost a hundred years! I had needed Abigail to get there. Maybe he needed *me*.

I needed to think, but first I needed to rest. Some food would have been extremely welcome, but currently it was not helpful to think about how satisfying a slice of pepperoni pizza would be. *Chewy crust. Stretchy cheese. Crispy meat discs.* Snap out of it, Stephen! Focus!

I looked around, wondering where I should settle down for the night. I plunked myself down right under the little amount of light that remained, directly under the steam clock. Anywhere else seemed too dark, too cold, and too spooky.

I laid my head down on my right arm and thought that this day had had its cool moments. As I tried to drift off to sleep, the day's events floated through my mind, like those speech bubbles in comics. *The museum, seeing Willy's wax statue, the treasure box, the steam clock . . .* My eyes drooped. *Mom.* Had she insisted that the entire police force come searching for me yet? *The realm of the dead, The Midway, The Great Sea, The Chasm.*

Mrs. Morris's words kept bouncing around my head too. She had said that I must be here for a reason. I believed her.

Fatigue started to overtake me. I peeked at my left arm. A little fuzzier, but still here. As I was trying to relax and sleep, I realized that something about my right arm felt off now. I opened and closed my hand a few times, and it was subtle, but I could still feel a twinge — the remains of the jolt that had radiated up my arm earlier in the day. Before I'd ended up here. When I was with Mom, in the museum. The moment I had touched William J. Sapperton's nameplate.

CHAPTER 14

My sleep was interrupted by a loud noise and a vibrating dirt floor. As quickly as I could gather myself, I sat up.

"What's that sound? Why is the ground shaking?" I asked aloud, rubbing my eyes. How long had I been asleep?

"It's just the steam clock," Abigail answered, hovering right beside me. "Don't worry about the trembling and such, it does this every day."

"How long have you been here?" I was somewhat startled.

"I just got here. Your head covering has fallen off." Abigail pointed at the ground behind me.

I smacked my dry lips together. I wished I had some lip balm. Or a sandwich. My breath was probably poisonous right now. I hoped ghosts had no sense of smell.

Groggily, I gathered myself. So I had made it through the night without fading away after all. But still, something felt *off*. My entire body felt like it was being pelted with an onslaught of frozen hail. The Midway trembled and hummed.

"It does this every day?" I asked Abigail. Little bits of dirt shook free from the walls and landed on top of my head.

"With the whistles from the steam clock," Abigail explained. "We hardly notice anymore."

"Where's Willy?"

"He's still there," Abigail whispered, pointing in his direction. I could barely make him out. His form was so nebulous, so faint.

The whistle from the steam clock seemed to ring loudly in my head. I winced and rubbed the skin on my arms to try to shake the prickly feeling. Above me, the tunnel of light surrounding the clock was dotted with the shadows of the people around it. The whole area seemed foggier, as if the mist from the clock was sinking down, reaching out like tendrils toward me.

Abigail reached out to touch the fog. "I don't remember seeing this happen before."

"How many whistles was that?" I stood up.

"I haven't been paying attention," Abigail confessed.

"The fog, creeping down like that. That's only happened once before," Willy said, slowly inching his way toward me. It was as though he was having trouble moving. "*The other one.* Is that what happened?" He wearily looked up to the steam clock.

My eyes popped open. Maybe this was it? Yesterday, precisely twenty-four hours ago — *this* was where it had all started. The noon whistle from the steam clock was the beginning. Was this my chance to go home?

"I think I'm leaving," I said, frozen on the spot.

"Now?" Abigail cried. "This can't be goodbye!"

The vapors from the steam clock started to blanket me. I couldn't move; I could only watch, wild-eyed. My skin danced and tingled *everywhere*, even in places I shouldn't talk about.

"Your head covering!" Abigail pointed furiously at my bandanna on the ground.

Any urge I had to lunge for it was quashed by fear of ruining my chance to get out of here.

Through the break in the misty clouds, I saw their faces. Abigail looked shocked and bewildered, while Willy's ghost trembled and flickered.

"He's leaving too," Willy mumbled, staring at the ground as his shoulders sagged.

I hated the idea of just leaving like this, so abruptly. It had only been a day, but I *liked* Abigail. She understood me. Despite the fact that she was a ghost, I considered her my friend. And Willy . . . while he was not exactly BFF material, part of me liked him too. I didn't like the idea that he'd soon be gone, like *really gone*. It didn't feel right.

Before I realized what I was saying, I pointed to my bandanna and yelled, "I'm coming back for it!"

My arm started to tingle again. I opened and closed my hand into a fist.

I shouted to Willy, "I won't let you down! I'm coming back to help you!" I didn't *want* to come back, but I felt I *should*.

The twelfth whistle sounded. I knew it was the last one — longer and louder than the others, with a forceful burst of fog that enveloped me completely, followed by a glaring flash.

All I could see was the vapor of the steam cloud. All I could feel was a gentle tingle on my arm. I turned my head from side to side, but the air was still too dense to see through. Strange voices surrounded me. I heard the sound of a car driving by, but it was clear and not muffled. The vapor was slowly dissipating, and there were some clear pockets where I could see faces of people looking at their cell phones. I could see the steam clock directly in front of me.

At first, my feet were firmly anchored to the ground, but as the steam cleared more, I began to look around and was able to take a few cautious steps away from the clock. Then the tap on my shoulder.

"You're back." Mom's voice.

I whipped around. The steam cloud was completely gone now, and I was looking directly into my mother's face.

"Mom!" I reached for her and threw my arms around her waist.

She let me hug her and I felt her arms wrap around my shoulders.

"Hi," she said simply.

I let go, and all the warm, fuzzy feelings I had had upon first seeing her gave way suddenly. I found myself feeling annoyed. "*Hi*? All you have to say is *hi*? How about 'I've been worried sick!' How about 'Where have you been?'"

She took a small step back and looked confused. "*Hi* is a very normal greeting." I couldn't help but notice she glanced up at my bandanna-less head.

"*A very normal greeting?*" I shouted. Oh sure, if your son hadn't been gone for a whole day it would have been normal, but this was *not* normal!

"Let's walk, shall we?" she suggested. Even though I was seething, mechanically, my legs started to follow her.

"I guess you haven't noticed that I've been gone for a whole day!"

"Really, Stephen. Don't be ridiculous. Of course I noticed." She kept her eyes straight ahead.

Suddenly, I stopped walking. There it was — Ye Olde Pasta Warehouse. Even down the block, the smell of garlic and tomato sauce had filled the air and grabbed me by the nostrils. "Lunch. Immediately." I pointed to the restaurant.

"Don't you want to go home? Clean yourself up a bit?"

"Food," I demanded firmly, arms crossed.

We were seated, and before the server — dressed in an old-fashioned shirt and skirt that looked a lot like what Mrs. Morris had been wearing — could even ask, I said, "I am extremely thirsty. I need an entire pitcher of water and the largest glass of lemonade you have."

While waiting for the drinks to arrive, Mom and I looked over the menu in silence.

I decided what I wanted. In fact, I wanted *everything*, but I held my greed in check. I slammed the menu down on the table.

She peered at me over her sheet. "The penne pesto chicken sounds good," she said.

"*The penne pesto chicken sounds good?*" I was back to loudly repeating everything she said and turning it into an angry question.

She opened her mouth just as our server returned with our drinks. I reached for the glass of lemonade, which was as tall as my forearm. I held the cold drink up to my lips and opened my mouth. I would have been drooling if I had had any saliva in my body to spare. When the liquid hit my tongue, I sighed, but I didn't stop. *Glug, glug, glug, glug, glug . . . ahhhh.*

I wiped my mouth with the back of my hand and Mom wrinkled her nose.

The server had been watching me the whole time with her mouth slightly open. "Ready to order?" she asked. I respected her professionalism.

"I'd like the manicotti with meat sauce and the fettuccini alfredo with shrimp."

"Both?" she asked, looking slightly surprised.

I nodded and glared at her, practically daring her to doubt me again. But like I said, she was a professional, and she quickly turned her attention to Mom.

"Penne pesto chicken, please." Mom handed over our menus.

The awkward silence began. I was waiting for Mom to say something, but it looked like she was waiting for me too.

It was a standoff. I poured myself another glass of water.

Glug, glug, glug, glug, glug . . . ahhhh.

Mom clamped her lips tight like a panini press. *Mmmm, panini.*

"Stephen," Mom started. I claimed a small victory! She yielded first.

I stared at her, trying to copy her best eyeball bulge.

"I'm glad to see you're okay." And that was it. The floodgates opened and all the things I had been holding back, due to severe dehydration, came rushing out.

"Don't you want to know where I was? I've been gone all day! All night! I could have been kidnapped! Did you even call the police?"

Mom sighed deeply. "I knew you were okay."

"*You knew I was okay?*" I repeated.

"I asked around."

"*You asked around?*"

"I knew exactly where you were."

"*You knew exactly where I was?* How is that possible?" If we had been at home, I would have been shouting at top volume, but here in the restaurant I found myself restraining my voice. Still, the veins on my neck were about to break through my skin.

Mom looked up at the ceiling. "This is not going well. I suppose it would all make more sense to you if I started at the beginning."

CHAPTER 15

Mom cleared her throat. "It behooves me to reveal that I am a mudang." She placed both of her hands flat on the table. "I'm not actively practicing, of course."

"What the heck is a mudang?" I asked impatiently, pouring myself a third glass of water.

"It's like a shaman — a person who connects with the gwisin." She paused and looked taken aback. "I haven't said that word in a long time. It's the Korean word for spirits."

"*You* connect with *spirits*?" I asked in disbelief. In her business suits and high-heeled shoes, she was the last person in Cedar Coast I would have guessed to be able to connect with anybody, dead or alive. "But you're a university professor!"

She looked annoyed. "One has nothing to do with the other."

I tapped my fingers on the table while I stared at her.

"Okay, so you're a mudang. And you connect with spirits," I said. "What does that even *mean*?"

She avoided looking at me for a moment before she answered. "Well, it *means* that those who have departed this mortal world are not necessarily departed for us. It's quite vexing, if I'm being honest."

"*Us*? What does this have to do with me?"

"It has everything to do with you. These sorts of spiritual abilities are often passed down. I had actually thought your father's ancestry would have stopped it from passing on to you — in fact, I was hoping for that — but it only appears to have delayed its appearance."

"I'm a mudang too?" My voice cracked and my mouth went dry.

"Well, for men, it's baksu mudang, usually just abbreviated to baksu. You are a baksu by birth, just as I was a mudang by birth, not choice. Certainly not by choice."

"Whoa." I let it all wash over me. A baksu by birth. I was *born* to talk to ghosts. Well, duh, that explained *a lot* about the last twenty-four hours. I smacked myself on the forehead.

The realization that I had had *this thing* in me my whole life, well . . . this just rocked my entire universe, didn't it?

"So, all our ancestors in Korea were mudangs too?" I asked. "Like, your parents and grandparents?"

Mom had never really talked about her family much. During the holidays or on birthdays, I only ever saw Dad's relatives. I hardly knew anything about the Ohs. All I knew was Mom had lived in Cedar Coast for about twenty-five years and that her mother, the one we only had a single picture of, had died a long, long time ago.

At least that's what Mom had told me. But there were a lot of things that she had "forgotten" to tell me about. Things like, "Our family talks to ghosts, Stephen." Important stuff like that!

Mom nodded. "It's usually passed down through the female line. Baksus are actually pretty rare."

We fell silent and our food just happened to arrive. The server put down little side plates of salad before placing our dishes of glorious pasta in front of us. I give Ye Olde Pasta Warehouse five stars for speed. Mom picked up her fork, stabbed a penne noodle, and chewed slowly.

I cut my manicotti down the middle and tried to shove one half in my mouth. Being a baksu was cool and all, but even a baksu needed to eat.

"So, is *that* why I got taken to The Midway? I'm *supposed* to connect with ghosts?" I asked as sauce dribbled down my lip. Was Mrs. Morris right? Was that the reason I was there?

"The Midway?"

"The place underneath the steam clock," I explained. "You know, the place I've been for the last twenty-four hours?" I could not hold back the biting exasperation in my voice.

"Oh, it has a name?" She looked away and stuck out her bottom lip slightly. "Well, that's not entirely correct. 'The Midway,' as you call it, sits atop a high-energy spot. A kind of spiritual hotbed. You combine that with the noon sun, and whatever vein of geothermal energy they tapped into when they built the steam clock and, well, it's a very extraordinary location. Similar spots, minus the steam clock, are scattered throughout the world, sometimes in unexpected places like mountains, sometimes in caves. I've even heard of one that was underneath a highway overpass. Oh dear, I find it quite annoying when words fail me. How can I describe it? It's a place for . . ." She stared at the table.

"Waiting," I suggested, remembering what Abigail had told me.

"It's a bit more complicated than that, but as a summary that would do. But the living are not supposed to be there. It is a place for spirits."

She had that right. I stared at the back of my hands. My body, thankfully, was looking more solid now.

I spooned the last of my manicotti into my mouth, pushed the plate to the side, and moved on to the fettuccini.

"Well, what do you *do*?" I asked her, slurping a noodle.

Looking confused, she replied, "I teach undergraduate students. But you *know* that already, Stephen."

I rolled my eyes. "No, no! With the spirits. What do you *do* with them?"

"What do I *do*?" she asked, startled. "I suppose historically a mudang is meant to act as a go-between of sorts. A listener, a helper. Sometimes spirits are troubled and need to talk. Sometimes a person in this world needs to reach out to a departed soul to settle something. Usually *emotions*. You shouldn't get involved in *that* type of interaction at all. Very precarious."

I realized I was listening so intently that I was sitting there with a mouthful of pasta that I hadn't swallowed.

She continued. "Each spirit needs something different. However, I do nothing with the spirits. Over the years, I've tried my best to ignore them. I'm quite good at it."

The hand waving across her face. I gulped down my food. "By doing this?" I mimicked her.

"I don't do that!" She looked offended.

"Oh, yes you do!"

"*Humph.*" She snorted. "Well ... I just don't want anything to do with it. It was never something I wanted."

Typical. Give her cool abilities and she *wastes* them! Mom was so aggravating.

I pushed my empty plate away, but I was still so hungry, I even decided to eat my salad.

"Mom. I have so many questions. But can we talk about it later? I'm dead." Poor word choice. "I mean, I'm exhausted." I had TMI overload.

"Of course. I'm rather tired myself. Let's go home."

I really wanted to pepper Mom with questions on the drive home, but my mouth wouldn't work. Every time I opened it to ask something, I found I couldn't get it out. Instead, her words just kept dancing around in my head.

Spirits. Baksu. Go-between. Listener. Helper.

When we got home, I took a long shower. Maybe the longest I'd taken in my entire life. I flicked shampoo bubbles around me while the hot water pelted my back. I would never take running water for granted again.

The conversation with Mom had been a lot to take in. She was a mudang. I was a baksu. Why didn't she care about having this *gift?* My heart swelled when I thought about it.

What did it all mean? Me and the ghosts. Abigail, her mother, and Willy. Mom said I wasn't supposed to have been there, and the fact that my body parts had started to slowly disappear confirmed that that was definitely true. But somehow, I had been there anyway.

After running a towel over my wet hair, I suddenly thought about the bandanna that I had left in The Midway. Thank goodness Dad had bought me an extra one last month. He had said something about the other one being "ripe" — I disagreed but promised him I'd wash them at least once a month. But we all tell little white lies, don't we, Dad? Things like, "I'll take you sailing again, don't worry."

I stepped into the kitchen, freshly washed and with a clean bandanna tied around my head.

"Oh," Mom blurted out when she saw me. She was sitting at the table, holding a cup of hot tea between her hands.

"Oh what?" I asked.

Her eyes darted to the top of my head. "I thought maybe . . . Never mind."

"Sorry to disappoint you, but I left the other one in The Midway by accident. This is my backup. And yes, it's from Dad." I pointed to my head.

She made her I-just-sucked-a-lemon face.

"Can we talk?" I asked, pulling up a chair to sit next to her. My energy had returned.

She blew gently across the top of her hot cup. "Of course."

"So, I'm a baksu. How can I help? You know, the ghosts? You said mudangs and baksus were helpers. Why else would we have these abilities? It must be for a bigger purpose. A reason."

Her shoulders slouched. "You're twelve. How can you possibly help?"

I bristled. "Willy needs help. Maybe I could, you know, help him. Somehow?" I felt my cheeks grow hot.

"Willy?" she asked with her brows furrowed.

"He's one of the ghosts I met. You know, that guy who got shipwrecked here? Captain William J. Sapperton. Although he's pretty casual and said I should just call him Willy. Also, Abigail Morris! She was really nice. And her mom, and there was this one creepy guy, but I don't want to talk about him."

She stared into her cup before she said, "Stephen, as a person with some experience in these matters, I think it's best that you just forget it all happened."

My mouth dropped open.

"It was just a mistake. Remember, you weren't supposed to be there."

Mistake or not, how could I forget? I would *never* forget.

"But he's trapped and has Transcendent Affliction!" I protested.

"Transcendent Affliction? What on earth is that?"

"He . . . cries," I said. But I realized right away that wasn't a good description.

"Everybody cries," Mom said dismissively.

"No, this was something else. This was . . ." I paused, not knowing if I could describe it. "An ache so deep it reverberated throughout The Midway and beyond to

The Great Sea. His time is almost up," I told her, my voice fading.

"That's a rather overdramatic description, don't you think? Anyway, what can you *do* about it, Stephen? I recommend that you just follow my example and live your life without all the ghosts. Forget about the dead. Just live."

Her words shocked me.

How could I *just live* when she'd just told me that I was born to talk to ghosts and to help them!

"Never mind!" I pushed myself away from the table and stomped to my room. She had decided a very long time ago to stop listening to the spirits, and she had no interest in being a mudang.

I didn't need her advice. It was pretty obvious that this baksu was going to find his own way.

CHAPTER 16

Even though I was still suspended and couldn't go to school, Mom let me meet Brandon after he got dismissed. She had abandoned her great educational plans, and we'd both spent most of the day staring at computers or TVs. *Battleships of Space* was kind of boring by myself, but I still played until my thumbs hurt.

I hadn't talked anymore about The Midway, and the only thing she had said to me today was, "What do you want for lunch?" It was like she wanted to pretend that everything was normal. But it would never be normal again. Not for me, anyway. She could pretend all she wanted, but I needed somebody to talk to. This was not the kind of information you shared by text message, and it definitely couldn't wait until I went back to school tomorrow.

Brandon and I decided to meet up on the seawall near the marina. I cycled to our meeting spot nervously. I had *so* much to tell him.

I was there first, and I waited on an empty bench. *Blackbeard's Vestige* was still gone. Of course it was still out — what kind of an adventure can you have over just a couple of days? Still, I missed the sight of it, and hoped that it would soon return, grimier than before, with secrets of the adventures it had just had locked away in the boat's memory.

Brandon rounded the curve in the seawall bike path. I had never been so happy to see him. Unlike Mom, I knew he'd be excited about everything that had happened to me.

As soon as he saw me, he flashed an exaggerated smile. His teeth looked even whiter than before!

His bike skidded to a halt.

"Check out my temporary teeth!" he proclaimed, smiling broadly.

I didn't know how to feel about the situation. This was my fault, but he seemed unbothered.

"Was it expensive?" I asked sheepishly.

"Mom's got a good dental plan. I don't think it was too bad."

"I've got some money saved up. Can I help pay?" I asked.

"Come on." He shook his head. "It was an accident. It could have easily been me breaking your finger or something. It's fine. Parents need to realize that children are expensive and unpredictable."

I agreed gratefully.

He sat down next to me, took off his helmet, and ran his hand through his hair. "So, what have you been up to?" he asked innocently.

The whole story gushed out of me, mostly in order but not always. I told him everything — about being sucked below the steam clock, and the ghosts I'd met, and how as soon as I'd got back, Mom told me that I was a baksu. By the time I was finished, it felt like I had been talking for an hour straight.

"This is so dope!" Brandon slapped my shoulder. "You have … *powers!*" He stood up from the bench and shouted at nobody in particular. "My best friend has powers!"

"*Shh!*" I grabbed his shirt and pulled him back down.

His mouth and his eyes were opened wide, and he just continued to stare at me in disbelief.

"I know, it's a lot, right?" I sighed.

I could see him thinking. "Wait, there's something I don't get. Why *now*? Why haven't you talked to ghosts before?"

I stopped to think. "I don't know. Mom said something about my dad's genes delaying it." I shrugged.

"Or did something *happen* to you?" He pushed loose curls off his forehead, and I could see his eyes gleaming as he tried to puzzle it out. I couldn't tell if he was joking or not.

"What do you mean?"

"My mom's been into sort of, what's it called? You know that stuff Ms. Atwal has us do? Mindfulness?" he explained. "You know, with the baby coming and all that, she's trying to be more aware of her body."

I stared at Brandon quizzically as he continued.

"She has high blood pressure from the pregnancy. She's been trying all kinds of things, seeing lots of different kinds of doctors, doing lots of different kinds of exercise. She's convinced that she needs to have more positive energy flow."

My eyebrows shot up.

"She's still working on it." Brandon chuckled quietly. That was obvious.

We fell silent for a while. Just for a second, I closed my eyes and tried to imagine *my* energy flow.

"Once she has positive energy flow, she thinks her body will be healthier."

"Really?"

"Yeah. The human body can be amazing, but we don't really pay enough attention to what our bodies tell us. It's all about concentrating and being aware. She thinks stress is blocking her positive energy flow, so she's trying to let it all go."

Ms. Atwal said stuff just like that just before our Mindful Minute. This whole time, I thought she just wanted an excuse to keep us quiet for one dang minute.

"Everything has energy flow. Even this bench." He gave the wood a tap.

"Everything?" I started to think.

He nodded. "Yup. Did you do anything unusual to cause a change or something like that?"

I sat up straighter. "You know, at the museum, when I touched part of the box that belonged to Willy, I *felt* something." I hesitated and didn't mention that I sort of *damaged* the box. "It was the first time I noticed it, anyway." I flexed my forearm, remembering the tingly feeling. "Then weird prickles kept happening!"

"That makes total sense!" Brandon sat up. "It once belonged to him. You felt his *energy*. Maybe even a little bit of him passed to you, like a kind of cosmic connection." He looked solemn. "This is bigger than you can imagine."

"You think?" I asked. "Mom thinks it was all just a mistake."

"No, I don't believe that for a second. It's like you were meant to meet him," Brandon said with uncharacteristic seriousness. "And you did."

"Whoa," I whispered. I *did* end up in The Midway, even though it was not a place for the living. Mistake or not, it seemed pretty important.

"Our oath," Brandon said suddenly, clutching my forearm.

"What about it?"

"The last line." He held up a finger.

"*Adventure is our fate,*" we both said at the same time.

He slapped my shoulder again. "Bro! *This* is your adventure! The one you're meant to have. It's like a game of Tetris where all the pieces are coming together perfectly!" He spread the fingers on his hands wide apart, and then he interlaced them.

I was too stunned to speak.

"All this time, I was listening to my mom babble on and on about conscious breathing and vital energy flows at dinner, and honestly, I had my doubts, but it turns out she might have been onto something." He paused. "*We* might also have been onto something ages ago. Like, how did we know you could talk to ghosts when we wrote the oath? Are we psychic?" Brandon asked as he held a serious look for about four seconds before he burst out laughing.

His laugh was infectious. We sat on the bench clutching our stomachs from laughing so hard before I realized I was tired of sitting.

"Come on, my butt's on fire from sitting too long," I told him, standing up and stretching out my back. "I'm not sure we'll ever figure out why this is happening. But it *is*."

"Let's change it up. My butt hurts too. You *definitely* need more practice with sword fighting." He smiled at me with all of his teeth. "Let's go to the park. We can find some sticks. Small ones, though!" Brandon stared at me playfully.

"Very, very small," I agreed. I did not want Mrs. Markovich's blood pressure to explode.

We picked up our bikes and headed over to the park not too far away. It had a large grove of trees.

I wasn't sure if I had a special connection with Willy, but it sure would have explained a lot. Not that anything made much sense these days. A baksu definitely had a purpose, though. Otherwise, what was the point of being able to talk to ghosts?

Brandon dropped his bike on the grass and ran for the trees, and I followed. We scoured the ground and managed to find a few decent-looking twigs. I held one in my right hand briefly before I snapped my wrist to see how it would parry.

It had been a few days since I had practiced my footwork, and while Brandon was still looking for his perfect stick, I began to practice my basic linear passing step. I did it twice and was preparing to give it a third go when the twig pulled away from my hand, sailed several feet, and struck Brandon in the back.

"Hey!" Brandon shouted. "What did you do that for?" He turned around and glared at me.

My jaw dropped. "I . . . I didn't do that!"

"What do you mean?" He took a few steps closer to me. He had started to get mad about being hit, but the look on my face must have changed his mind, and now he seemed a little worried.

"The stick just ... flew out of my hand," I said, dumbfounded. A frigid wind brushed my shoulder, and all the hairs on the back of my neck stood up. The ends of the knot in my bandanna were pulled to the side. I lurched around to see who had done that.

"*Nice to see you again.*" The words were faint and barely audible. I swiveled around quickly, trying to make sense of what was happening. Out of the corner of my eye, I saw a flash of a face — a familiar face with a scar that hadn't healed. The air around me felt misty and cold.

"The gwisin are here," I said breathlessly.

CHAPTER 17

As calmly as I could, I said to Brandon, "Get your bike. We have to leave."

"What's going on?"

"The gwisin . . . I mean, the *ghosts*." I shook my head, realizing that I was using the Korean word Mom had taught me. I had only just learned it, so of course Brandon wouldn't know what it meant. "One of them is here. I met him in The Great Sea. He's not the kind you want to meet more than once!" This baksu business was way scarier than I had imagined.

Brandon gave me a quizzical look.

"Get your bike. I'll tell you as we walk."

With my heart pounding firmly against my ribs, I took a deep breath and gathered my things.

"When I made it to The Great Sea with Abigail, there was this spirit. Not a spirit like Abigail either. He had this scar on his face that looked like it had never healed properly. How can I describe it?" I closed my eyes and remembered. "Kind of . . . oozy?"

Brandon cringed.

"I never found out his name, so in my head I named him Sliced Cheek."

"Sliced Cheek?" Brandon shuddered.

"He just felt . . . dangerous. I didn't get that feeling from anybody else down there."

"So that guy, he's *here*?"

"Yes, he just talked to me." My legs moved at high speed. Making a grave error, I glanced back to see that Sliced Cheek wasn't alone. There were several spirits hovering together. I was *not* about to stop and take a good look at them, though.

"What?" Brandon stopped in his tracks.

"Keep walking!" I said, eyes firmly ahead of me.

"Sliced Cheek talked to you *just now*?" Brandon jogged to catch up to me.

My bike suddenly felt like it weighed one thousand pounds.

"Yes." My voice was shaking. "He's not alone either. Get on your bike!"

Brandon and I stopped to jump onto our bikes, and the spirits, I don't even know how many, swirled around us. Like a powerful, blustery wind, they kept pushing us off balance.

"What's happening?" Brandon was struggling to keep his bike steady.

"Go away!" I yelled. I gripped my handlebars tight and closed my eyes.

"Just thought we'd say hello," Sliced Cheek whispered in my ear.

I swear my heart stopped. The blowing wind suddenly died down.

"Okay, what the heck just happened?" Brandon asked, completely bewildered.

He hadn't *seen* the spirits, but he had *felt* their malicious energy.

"You okay?" he asked as he pedaled alongside me.

"Let's just get out of here." I just wanted to get home — fast. I pedaled harder.

All of a sudden, it hit me. I understood why Mom didn't want to do this. Maybe this was my fate, but when a group of nasty ghosts starts following you home, it doesn't feel like an adventure anymore. It feels like a haunting. Being a baksu meant that I couldn't pick and choose who came to me. When I met ghosts like Abigail, it was great! She was nice and had no desire to terrorize me. But this Sliced Cheek guy? I wasn't sure what he was capable of doing — honestly, I didn't want to find out. Maybe being a baksu wasn't so awesome after all.

Since I'd got back from my ghost encounter in the park, I had mostly been sitting on the sofa with a box of cold Korean fried chicken perched between my chest and my stomach. Mom was letting me get away with all sorts of things today, and as long as I vacuumed up the crumbs after I was done, she was going to let me eat dinner riding the sofa while watching TV. These were unprecedented times.

I'd hardly spoken since I'd seen Sliced Cheek. Mom probably thought I was just mindlessly staring at the TV, but I wasn't even paying attention — I was still thinking about that face.

How could I *not* think about Sliced Cheek? He was hard to forget. Next time, although I really hoped there wouldn't *be* a next time, I was going to try that thing Mom did and wave my hand across my face.

I practiced it. I tried it at slow speed: one hand swipe to the left, one hand swipe to the right. Nope. Not good enough for a ghost like Sliced Cheek. Then I tried it double-time, with twice as many hand flicks. Four hand flicks, and fast. This seemed like it might work on a malevolent ghost . . . and possibly mosquitoes.

The box of chicken was empty except for the last little bits of crispy coating littering the bottom, and I finally got up to throw it away. But not before I tipped the corner of the box into my open mouth and let all the last crumbly bits cascade down like a waterfall of deep-fried rain.

It was getting late, and I was more than ready to go to bed. Just before I stepped into my room, Mom shouted, "Crumbs!" from somewhere in the apartment.

Right. I guess I had told her I'd clean up, so I needed to vacuum. A promise is a promise.

CHAPTER 18

I curled up and reached for *Treasure Island*, hoping it might make me feel better. Sometimes I would just open to a random page and start reading. But tonight, I found I couldn't focus. Instead, I closed it and put it back on my bedside table without reading a single word. Never did I think I'd say this, but today, I wasn't in the mood for Long John Silver or tales of treasure. I was in the mood for normal things, like sleeping. I flicked the switch of my lamp and soon, my eyelids slammed shut.

Sleep came to me quickly, but it was interrupted. I awoke shivering under my blanket. When I peeked out from beneath my heavy eyelids, I saw that the window, which was usually kept open just a crack to let in cool air, had been blown wide-open.

I sat up groggily. Leaning over to close the window, I felt a tug on my T-shirt. Then I heard it. It was a chant. Barely audible, so I closed my eyes to listen carefully. It was the quietest and coldest of whispers. "*A promise made is a promise that must be kept.*"

"But I vacuumed the crumbs," I murmured.

Again, I heard it. "*A promise made is a promise that must be kept.*" This time, the voice was louder. I felt my brain spring to attention. It wasn't Mom chastising me for making a mess at all. Wide awake now, I knew it was Sliced Cheek. He was back, and he was in my *room*. He wasn't alone either. Just like in the park, there were other ghosts flanking him.

I summoned any courage I had, and I found myself shouting, "Get out of here! I didn't make any promises!"

Suddenly, his face was inches from me. Too terrified to move, I stared at his cold, lifeless figure. How different he was from Abigail! Even though she was a spirit too, she was gentle and kind. Sliced Cheek was nothing like her. Meeting my gaze, his villainous eyes gave the smallest of glints, but there was no warmth.

I froze for a second before I remembered and tried the hand flicking technique. *Double-time!* I reminded myself as I batted my hand across my face quickly.

Sliced Cheek laughed cruelly. The other spirits had moved next to him, and the four of them chuckled alongside.

"Come now, you think ghosts like us will go away so easily?" His voice was now clear and distinct, as it had been in The Midway.

I gulped.

"We decided to pay you another little visit. A little *friendly* reminder," he hissed.

"What are you talking about?" My teeth chattered.

"See, boys? I told you. The live ones have short memories." The others nodded in agreement. "I'm here on a noble mission of sorts."

"What do you want?" I couldn't stop my voice from trembling.

"Captain Willy told me that just before you left The Midway, you promised him you'd be back. You haven't forgotten, have you?" Sliced Cheek pulled away from me slightly and floated around my room.

"Were you one of Willy's *crew*?" I asked tensely.

"You insolent brat. He's a *captain*!" a ghost with a long ponytail chimed in. He wore a heavy chain around his neck and his face was covered in a rough beard.

"But, but . . ." I stammered. "He said to just call him Willy."

The ghosts all paused. Sliced Cheek and the others glanced at each other quickly.

"Once a captain, always a captain," Sliced Cheek said smoothly.

"Did he send you here?" I asked.

"No, he didn't send me. He's given up." Sliced Cheek looked at his fingernails. "He was once a proud captain, he was. Firm, but with a little bit of rum in him, he could spin a yarn!"

"You caused my captain to have Transcendent Affliction. The least you could do is try to make it right," the bearded ghost said. "He was the best of captains! He took me on board when everybody else turned me away!"

"Without Captain Willy, I'd have lost both," a gruff ghost spoke as he pointed to his missing eye. He didn't even wear an eyepatch over the empty socket. The seam along the shoulder of his tattered vest looked to be held together by a thin bone. I sure hoped it was from a chicken.

"So..." I managed to choke out. "What do you want me to do about it?"

"We don't know why it's you. We don't really care, quite honestly. You have the ability to do something," Sliced Cheek said calmly.

"He's scrawny! Mate, are you sure he can do anything?" another ghost asked Sliced Cheek. This one was missing a hand. His clothes were in worse shape than Sliced Cheek's.

"Oh, he's the one all right," Sliced Cheek replied to his friend. He never took his eyes off me. "You might say it runs in the family."

He squinted his eyes and a dimple emerged on his one good cheek. There was a distinct difference between a comforting smile and a threatening one.

I felt all the blood drain from my face.

"Do what you said you would and help him. His time's almost up. We haven't the luxury of waiting around." Sliced Cheek paused. "Or perhaps you'd like me to stay awhile, until you have a change of heart?" He glanced around the room casually.

"Do you know how insufferable Transcendent Affliction sounds, even to the likes of us?" the pirate with the missing hand said. "My head's still ringing! And it's all your fault!" He pointed the stump of his arm at me.

I opened my mouth to reply, but just at that moment, my bedroom door flew open. In the doorway stood my mother wearing a bathrobe, her hair rolled into a towel on top of her head, and on her face a semi-transparent Korean beauty sheet mask. I wasn't sure who was scarier right now, her or Sliced Cheek.

"Away!" she bellowed with an intensity I had never heard from her before. She waved her right arm broadly. It was an amplified version of the face swat she always did. The movement of her arm seemed to send a powerful current through the air. The force pushed Sliced Cheek and his mates back. They recoiled slightly, but they also recovered quickly. Once Sliced Cheek regained his balance, he started to laugh defiantly.

"That was a nice tickle," he replied, flying straight up into Mom's face. "Do it again."

Mom's face fell and she tried waving them away again, with even less effect. All the ghosts were laughing at her now. The look of despair on her face was unmistakable, even from under the sheet mask.

"Not as much influence as you think, eh, miss?" said the ghost with the ponytail as he hovered uncomfortably close to her face.

"I know it's been a while, but what happened to you?" the one-eyed crewman mocked. "You couldn't send away a gnat, could you?"

"What do you say, boys? Do they need a little encouragement?" Sliced Cheek taunted us.

These were the worst kind of pirates. Menacing and cruel. I wanted nothing to do with the likes of these spirits. I remembered why I had chosen to be a piventurate instead. A piventurate wanted none of this meanness, only adventure! My heart sank down to my kneecaps.

In a flash, the crew swirled around my room, their movements frenzied and chaotic. I cowered in my bed, my arms over my head.

Mom sat down beside me and threw her arm over my shoulders. "Help me send them away."

Our eyes locked. "Focus," she said firmly. "Use your arm, like I just did. You can do it. On three." She looked calm even as she put her hands up to protect her face, but I knew there was an edge of fear in her voice.

She held out her index finger as the ghostly crew tossed the papers from my desk and knocked over my pirate lamp. She then held out a second finger, and I tried to sit up straighter in my bed. I wasn't sure this was going to work. I had already tried the quick hand motion, and it hadn't done a thing. She hadn't been able to get rid of them the two times she'd tried either.

But they were destroying my room! *Treasure Island* flew by me and landed on the floor. I stared in dismay as I watched the spine of the book, my favorite book, split into two. Had they no respect for classic pirate lore?

I clenched my right hand and dug my nails deep into my palm. I pushed out all the fear as best I could. Then Mom held out a third finger.

I threw my arm like a backhand shot across my body and shouted with all my strength. "Away!" we bellowed together.

The ghosts, all five of them, were thrown back to the edges of the room. They seemed surprised. So was I! The air around us felt different. It grew calm.

Sliced Cheek, now pushed farther away from my bed, smiled mischievously and flew slowly toward the open window. "You were always an unpleasant one," he told Mom. Then he looked at me and said, "Remember what we talked about, young Stephen." He winked. "Mates, I think we need to move on to the next stage.

This one might need a little more *persuading*," Sliced Cheek said ominously to his crewmates. Several of them smiled chillingly.

"A little motivation!" they chanted together.

"We know how to do that, don't we, boys?" another of his crew cackled. He hadn't spoken before. He was the largest of the group — a bald spirit, covered in tattoos. Even on his *face*. Skulls and crossbones on both cheeks.

I felt faint and goosebumps erupted all over my arms. What on earth did they mean by that?

A chill swirled around me as they all flew out the window. The room was finally still and free of ghosts.

Mom rushed over to close the window and then sat on my bed next to me. "Are you okay?" she asked.

Stiff as a plank, I nodded yes.

She ran her hand over my cheek and said, "Most of them aren't like that."

"I know," I whispered, thinking of Abigail.

Having Mom look back at me from behind a sheet mask was creeping me out. "Can you take that thing off?" I pointed to her face.

"Oh, right." She peeled it away. "What happened before I came into the room? Why did they visit?"

"They said they want me to help Willy." I put my hand on my chest and tried to calm my nerves.

"Willy? Why do they care?"

"He was their captain." They were a loyal crew, I'd give them that.

Mom did not reply, and I could not read the look on her face.

"They told me I had the ability to do something. To help," I said, wondering how we'd finally managed to get rid of them. "While there is still time."

"Now, you will do no such thing. You'll have to learn how to better ignore their voices. It will come with practice," Mom said firmly.

"But you couldn't ignore them or get rid of them at first," I ventured. "Haven't you been practicing for a long time?"

She looked displeased. But I was right, wasn't I? I suddenly realized that she hadn't been able to get rid of them without *me*.

"Maybe my skills *are* a little rusty," she admitted. "Plus, that kind are especially stubborn. When they come together like that for a single purpose, they can be powerful."

"You mean the really bad ones?" I murmured.

I glanced around my room, which was a mess. Paper everywhere, books tossed.

"Yes, the really bad ones." Her voice was as soft as I had ever heard it. "You *have* to ignore them."

"But I made Willy a promise. Kind of. They came to . . . remind me." *I won't let you down! I'm coming back to help you!* I had told him. "Doesn't my word count for something?"

"Now really, you needn't feel compelled to follow through with everything. You know how people always say things like, 'We should go out for dinner,' but they never actually invite you to dinner? It's one of those sorts of situations. Think of it as vacuous conversation — well-intentioned, I'm sure, but nobody is going to hold you to your word should you not actually fulfill your supposed promise." She sounded more like herself. As she got up, she patted my leg. "You're just a child, after all."

I nodded dully. I wanted to believe her, but I also got the feeling that Sliced Cheek and his friends weren't the type to just forget about things. They seemed like men who didn't make empty promises. If they wanted me to help Captain Sapperton, they could have asked *nicely* instead of threatening me. Some pirates have no manners.

"Try to get some sleep," Mom suggested as she leaned over to pick up some papers off the floor before heading to the door to turn off my light.

Sleep? Not likely! I turned my lamp back on and stared at the ceiling.

This was so hard. Could I hop into a time machine and go back to the days when Brandon and I had pretended we were piventurates in training — when our biggest problem was finding the right sized sticks for sword fighting? That was when I couldn't see or talk to ghosts.

Being a baksu was something I was born with. Being a piventurate was something I *wanted*. Maybe the two weren't so different after all. I was a baksu with the heart of a piventurate. It was my fate. It was right there in the Piventurate's Oath!

We draw no blood
We play as one
We never give up
'Cause quitting's no fun
We keep our word
We are best mates
Piventurates for life
Adventure is our fate

But oh, my Jolly Roger, my heart was scared. If I thought about it, though, I couldn't deny the other feeling either. Underneath all the fear, there was definitely a tiny tingle of excitement. A true piventurate couldn't just quit and run away from all this. I couldn't pretend I didn't hear voices like Mom did. Could I?

Gulp. My knees were knocking, but I forced myself out of my bed. Some pages had come loose during the haunting, and I gathered them up as best I could, but my torn copy of *Treasure Island* just wasn't the same anymore. It was ruined. I tucked the broken book into a desk drawer.

I was going to have to go back to The Midway. Definitely. Maybe. Probably? I mean, I had no clue what to *do* when I was there, but doing *nothing* didn't seem like an option. Oh, heck, I'd make my mind up in the morning. I'd just been attacked by evil spirits. How could I possibly make a decision under these conditions?

CHAPTER 19

Mom didn't seem herself the next morning. She couldn't fool me. I could see how tired she was. Maybe she didn't get any sleep either. We didn't say much to each other. She didn't even need to ask me to clean my room, which was trashed from all the chaos the ghosts had caused. As I'd had nothing to do at four in the morning, I had tidied my room then. It was as if the ghosts had never been there. Except I knew that they *had*.

I watched her carefully as we silently ate breakfast. Normally, she took confident strides around the apartment, even in her bathrobe. She was probably like that at work too — commanding the room when she taught classes. It was easy to imagine her standing at a lectern with everybody listening. But this morning was different. She seemed . . . smaller. Like less of herself.

Even though I had an hour before school started, I was getting my backpack organized. After missing most of the week, I couldn't believe I was actually not hating the idea of seeing everybody again. Except James. I always hated seeing James.

While I was making sure I had my spare eyepatch packed, my hand automatically ran up to the top of my head. My bandanna. Right. It seemed like a lifetime ago that I had silently raged at Mr. Huntington when he'd told me I wasn't allowed to wear it to school anymore. I ripped it off my head and threw it on top of the hallway table.

The knock at the door surprised me. In our building, nobody randomly came to the door, because you needed to be buzzed in by calling through the intercom system. Plus, it wasn't even eight o'clock yet. I looked down the hallway to see if Mom had heard it. I didn't hear her coming, so I tentatively got up and looked through the peephole.

It was Dad! I threw open the door and jumped into his arms.

"Dad!" I yelled.

Seeing him was such a surprise. I thought about all the things I needed to tell him, but where did I start? Chronologically? Or should I just jump to the really cool stuff, like I'm a baksu? Instead, I found that all I could do was give him a goofy grin, because when you don't see your dad for a while, it's sometimes hard to start a conversation, even if you have a giant boatload of things you need to say.

He was dressed casually, in a pair of loose jeans and a striped sweater. His light brown hair was slicked back. He gave my hair a rub and didn't say anything about my not wearing it, but I caught him glancing at the bandanna on the table. When he smiled, behind his glasses he had dark circles under his eyes, like he'd been staring at a computer screen for too long.

"Christopher," Mom said dryly. I hadn't heard her walking up. She scratched at her neck before crossing her arms in front of her chest.

"Minah," he replied, shifting his weight between his feet. He cleared his throat.

My eyes darted from Dad to Mom. How were these two ever married, I wondered. I didn't notice when I was really little, but lately it occurred to me that I didn't look like either of them. My hair was darker than Dad's, but not as dark as Mom's. I had Dad's cheekbones but

Mom's nose. My eyes were brown, but not dark brown like Mom's. I guess not every kid is the spitting image of their parents, but you always do have little bits of them with you. You just can't choose which parts.

"I still have the key fob for the building," he explained, even though neither of us had asked. "I've been meaning to give it back." He placed it down on the hallway table.

"What brings you here?" she asked calmly. "We have to get going shortly."

"I know, I know. School day. Can I come in?"

Mom dipped her head slightly. "I thought you were unable to fulfill your legal and moral obligation to take custody of your son this weekend."

He slumped. Mom had a way of making him lose all muscle mass in his body. The small reusable shopping bag he had strung over his shoulder slipped down the length of his arm.

"I know. I'm sorry about that. I do have a bunch of important meetings this weekend." He rubbed the back of his neck.

"Why are you here, then?" Mom pressed.

"You're going to think I've lost it. Last night, I couldn't sleep. It was really strange. Like I kept hearing a voice every time I tried closing my eyes," Dad said.

I listened intently.

"You look tired, buddy," he said to me suddenly.

"So do you," I replied. I wanted to tell him *why* I was tired, but it seemed weird to just blurt out that I had been terrorized by ghosts last night.

"Well, anyway, I just sort of had to get up last night, and I got the feeling I had to find something. You know?"

"No, I haven't the faintest idea what you're talking about," Mom said in a relaxed tone.

He fingered the handles of the bag before passing it to Mom.

"I think these belong to you. I don't know why I had them. They were mixed in with some of our ... my things. In a box I had forgotten about. I think it might be a family heirloom of yours. They look old."

"Really, there was no rush to return it." Mom slowly reached for the bag. "Given your hectic schedule and all that."

"That's just the thing — I felt like I *had* to," Dad said, looking baffled. "I just thought I would not get anything else done today if I didn't get them to you right away. It's so weird, it was like I was hearing things." He shook his head slightly and laughed quietly at himself.

Mom kept her eyes on Dad for a long time before she turned her attention to the bag. She opened it carefully and peered inside. Then she slammed it shut.

"Well, that's great. Thank you!" Mom said hurriedly. "We need to get going now." I gave her a look because that wasn't true. We still had at least forty-five minutes before I had to leave for school.

"Um, okay." Dad looked awkward. "I guess I'll get going, then."

"You just got here!" I complained.

"I'll make it up to you." I'd heard *that* one before. I hated it when he didn't keep his word. "Double O Stephen." He stuck out a fist and waited for a fist bump.

"Don't call me that. I can't stand it," I told him as I glanced away.

"You should never hate your name, Stephen. It makes you who you are."

I half-heartedly returned the fist bump because it's rude to leave your dad hanging like that, but I added, "And *you* shouldn't say things when you don't really mean them."

Dad flinched.

Mom was smirking right behind me; I could feel it.

"Okay, okay, point taken," he said humbly.

"I'm still open to bribe gifts," I reminded him. "I've got my eye on a new T-shirt. I'll send you a picture."

"Got it." He grinned and looked like he was turning to leave.

Then the clanging in the walls started again, but this time it was louder. Much louder.

"Okay, Christopher, thanks for stopping by." Mom started to push him out the door.

"What's that noise?" he asked, confused.

"I think something is wrong with the pipes in the building," I told him.

"I'll call you," he said as Mom started to close the door on him. "For real."

I waved goodbye. He still had no idea that there was really important stuff going on in my life, but that's how it was sometimes now that we didn't live together full-time. The door shut and it was just me and Mom again.

The clanging became louder and more intense, and it didn't seem muffled anymore. Before, it had seemed as though it was maybe coming from inside the walls, but now it was . . . different.

"Mom, we have to call the building manager right away. It feels like something is going to blow. We don't want water everywhere. Or even worse, sewage!"

Instead of answering me, she clutched the bag Dad had given her.

I stared at her and then at the bag. Was the noise coming from *the bag*?

"Mom . . ." I started to say as I took a step forward. She took a step back.

"Follow me," she said.

"Are you going to call the building manager?" I trailed her to her bedroom.

"It's not the pipes," she answered flatly.

"What do you mean? How do you know?"

She placed the bag on her bed and then moved to the closet. Quickly, she reached inside and pulled something out. It was the metal plate she had been holding just a few days ago when I'd walked in on her the first time we'd heard the clanging. She placed the plate on the bed, next to the bag.

Mom took a deep breath, closed her eyes for a moment, and then put her hand inside the bag and pulled out a second plate that looked identical to the first one.

The plates were definitely brass. But now that I could look at them better, I realized they were more like flat bowls. Almost the same shape as a thin tambourine.

There were also small ropes I hadn't noticed before, like handles, threaded through two small holes on each of their edges.

She stared at the two plates before she reached into the bag to remove a small hammer of some kind. Suddenly pivoting on her heels, she headed back into the closet and squatted down. After rummaging for a few seconds, she found a second, identical hammer. They were actually more like small mallets, because the heads were wide and thick. She lined everything up on the bed before she turned to me and said, "I guess it's about time you met your grandmother."

CHAPTER 20

"Grannie O'Driscoll?" I asked. "I just saw her at Easter."

"No, your *other* grandmother."

I couldn't grasp her meaning immediately. But when I figured out what she meant, I gulped. "You mean, the *dead* grandmother I've never met?" I pointed in the general direction of her picture on the hallway table.

"I had the distinct feeling that she'd been trying to call me but couldn't quite get through for some reason. Something was off. I tried getting a hold of her too, but couldn't." Her eyes narrowed slightly as if she was thinking hard.

"You've been trying to reach my dead grandma?" I asked, bewildered.

"You'll probably want to call her 'Halmeoni.' I don't think she'll like 'Grandma' very much."

"I don't understand," I said, trying to pull myself together. "Why doesn't she — I mean, Halmeoni — just . . ." My voice cracked. "Come *fly* by?"

"Oh, she never liked to travel much," Mom said matter-of-factly. "Most ghosts like to stick close to home."

Mom seemed unusually relaxed and almost chatty.

"I had been wondering where the second one went. I *knew* I needed both," she said quietly. "That's why I couldn't get through. Of course your father had it . . ." She rolled her eyes.

"These kkwaenggwari have been in the family for a long time. They're a kind of small gong. Most commonly, they are used in a traditional folk dance. But our family has also used them as a way of sending out a call. A kind of kinetic energy, to communicate with the spirits."

Tentatively, she picked up one of the mallets and gazed at its head.

"The kkwaenggwari are usually used to call *to* spirits, not for the spirits to call *us*, but I guess she is both a mudang and a spirit. Perhaps she can do what she likes. She always was quite forceful." She put the mallet down.

"Does she talk to you much?" I asked nervously.

Mom looked embarrassed. "Well, we had a falling out a long time ago. That's why I came here. To get away from it all, that life. Or so I thought. I guess that expression 'You can run, but you can't hide' has some merit."

Her face seemed wistful, until she snorted.

"Life is full of unimaginable twists and turns." She shook her head gently. Touching the kkwaenggwari gently with the tip of her finger, she continued, "Usually one is for the master and the other," she paused as she held my gaze, "for the student."

I reached for the gong she held out for me. My eyes were like saucers.

"With both of them together, I think she'll be able to talk to us now. I'm sure she was trying before. Between the two of us, the energy will be amplified. She is rather far away. Hold it like this." Mom demonstrated how to hold it by the rope handle and suspend it in midair.

"Energy?" I asked.

"You've heard of the concept *qi*? It describes the vital energy that flows around us and through us."

"Brandon!" I exclaimed. "He was talking about it before!"

Mom looked surprised but continued. "Brass is often overlooked, metaphysically speaking, because it's an alloy and not a 'pure' element. People tend to think it's not a powerful metal. But that's not true. In the hands of a mudang or baksu, the reverberations and the energy sent out by brass interact with qi and bring . . ." She paused and the corners of her mouth turned up. "Truth."

Everything she said left me feeling breathless.

"Brass is known, by mudangs anyway, to open pathways of communication. The energy emitted from brass helps calm surrounding chaotic energies — in other words, ghosts — and gives them courage by showing them an authentic version of themselves." Mom suddenly looked self-conscious.

"Their truth," I whispered.

"Yes, the courage to see their truth."

I couldn't believe Mom had been hiding all this from me. I couldn't believe she would walk away from all this knowledge.

"But what about . . . ?" I pointed to my face and drew a line down my cheek. "I *definitely* did not call him.

He just showed up," I said, trying to make sense of how this all worked.

"Yes, there are many spirits that just like to arrive unannounced. Believe me, I know. But they're local. Your halmeoni is across an ocean. Communicating is much more difficult."

I gulped.

"Take a mallet and give it a tap. Let's see what happens."

"For real?" I asked, holding the kkwaenggwari in my hands. The gong felt surprisingly light. As I held it, it buzzed in my fingers.

"Yes, for real." She looked at me encouragingly.

"What do you think is going to happen?" I asked, a little bit afraid but also a little bit excited.

"I think she's going to pay us a visit."

Nothing happened at first. We hit our gongs and waited. The sound was a very distinctive metal clanging, followed by a reverberation that filled the room. The tone was shallow and rich at the same time. The air around me hummed. I waited impatiently for something, anything, to happen. We held the drums to face each other, so that the energy could bounce back and forth between the two.

Instead of the sound fading, as it should have after several seconds, the reverberations seemed to get louder. The space around me quivered, and I could feel ripples of energy around my body.

"*Ya!* What's wrong with you?!" a voice shouted. The sound startled me, and I almost dropped the kkwaenggwari.

A face appeared in the surface of the drum I was holding. It was hazy and indistinct, but there was definitely a Korean lady staring right at us. This was Halmeoni. There was a firm toughness about her features, like you wouldn't want to haggle with her at a market because you knew you'd lose. Mom had definitely inherited her don't-mess-with-me demeanor.

"Hello, Eomeoni," Mom said coolly.

"I've been trying to reach you for days!" Halmeoni wagged a finger at Mom. She still hadn't even said hello.

"I didn't have both kkwaenggwari until today," Mom replied. The corners of her mouth tensed.

"I know! I had to shout and dance like a silly old lady all day yesterday. Finally, that lazy husband of yours could hear me. Oh, my throat!" She stroked her hand down her neck.

I perked up. Somehow Halmeoni got Dad here? She could *do* that? I remembered him saying that he felt like he had to come over. That must have been her doing. She had a lot of power, for sure.

"He's not my husband anymore."

"Divorced?" Halmeoni asked, raising an eyebrow.

"Yes, Eomeoni. You're probably more ashamed of me than ever."

"Impossible to be more ashamed than I already am," she muttered. "Ah, that's why the two gongs were not together." She clicked her tongue and shook her head. "Modern divorce, split everything fifty-fifty, even family treasure!"

"Did you control his *mind*?" I blurted out before I realized that she might not even know who I was. "Oh, and hi, Halmeoni. I'm Stephen." I held the gong out in front of me and waved at her image.

"My grandson! What a nice boy! So big. Halmeoni so happy to see you!" When she looked at me, the angry scowl she had worn when talking to Mom faded. She smiled at me warmly. "Don't worry, I didn't control your dad. No, no, I plant an *idea*. He doesn't hear me too well. Just like your eomma." She threw Mom a look. "So, I guess you didn't teach him Korean?"

"Anyway, it's so very nice to see you after such a long time," Mom said with a thick layer of sarcasm. "Now, what can we do for you?"

"First, I wanted to talk to you last week because I knew Stephen was finally changing. I could feel it." She looked at me fondly.

"I have changed," I replied tentatively, surprised that Halmeoni somehow seemed to know before I did.

"Ah, good boy. You feel it." She nodded with a smile that scrunched her nose. "But that's old news. Things are different now! Not good, not good." Her face changed quickly and she glanced over her shoulder.

Although I was just holding the gong by the string, I felt warmth starting to radiate off the brass surface. Its warmth reminded me of the way The Nexus, which should have felt cold, emanated heat.

"Where did she go?" Mom asked suddenly as she peered deeper into my kkwaenggwari.

"She's still right there!" I told her, pointing to the surface of my gong, where Halmeoni looked back at me. I was surprised that suddenly Mom couldn't see her own mother.

"I . . . I don't see her anymore," Mom said quietly as she sat down on the bed. I wondered what on earth was happening to Mom. First, she couldn't get rid of Sliced Cheek and his crew without me, and now this?

"Uh? She doesn't see me anymore?" Halmeoni said, shocked. "Not good. You see me, right, Stephen?"

I nodded.

"I knew one day she'd lose touch with her energy. Worst time! Ah, thank goodness for you, my grandson!" She abruptly softened her tone. "I don't usually bother your mom. You know why, right?"

I nodded again.

"It's important you listen now." She held my gaze. "Yesterday, I was just wandering in the spirit world — we call it The Vast Sea . . ."

The place Abigail mentioned! "The place around here is called The Great Sea."

"Same, but different. Anyway, I was just minding my own business, talking to friends. Then, some very bad men — *very* bad men — came a long way to find me. They grabbed me. They have me now," she said chillingly.

It was impossible to keep my mouth closed.

"What's she saying?" Mom asked.

I told her.

"What does she mean, they *have her*?" Mom asked. "How is that possible?"

"By themselves, I can blow these spirits away with just one tiny flick of my baby finger. They are nothing. But together, with a goal, their power is very surprising." The look on her face was unmistakable — she was afraid.

"Have they hurt you, Halmeoni?"

"No, no, but they took away my *freedom*. I'm trapped. I don't know how they did it. I think I'm trapped in a ship. You know, the jail part."

I gasped and put my hand up to my mouth.

"They've trapped Halmeoni in the brig of a boat!" I told Mom.

Her eyes widened. She mouthed, "What?"

"Stephen, they want something. You must do as they ask and help . . . oh, what's his name?"

"*Captain* William J. Sapperton." It was a voice I knew well. A voice I wanted to forget. "Are you *motivated* now?" Sliced Cheek asked as he pushed his face through the gong.

CHAPTER 21

I dropped the kkwaenggwari instantly. When I picked it back up, they were both gone. Halmeoni and Sliced Cheek — *poof*, not there anymore.

"What happened?" Mom asked as she looked blankly at the gongs.

"It was *him*." I drew a line down my cheek. I stared at the kkwaenggwari, hoping he wouldn't be back.

Mom turned ashen and slowly closed her eyes.

"They're holding her hostage!" I said in disbelief. These men in life and death were pirates with a capital *P*. And that was *no* compliment.

Mom and I just stared at each other, not knowing what to do or what to say.

"She's stronger than they are. She'll manage," she finally said.

"What?" I shouted. "She told me they had *trapped* her. And that their power was surprising. We saw first-hand how powerful they are together! They trashed my room! How's she going to get out of that by herself?"

"What can I do?" Mom held open both palms. "You saw, I'm . . . not very in tune with the spirits anymore." Her voice faded and she slipped awkwardly from the bed to the floor.

"It's what you wanted, isn't it? Now look! You've got no abilities left when it's suddenly important! Are you even a mudang anymore?"

Mom held her head in her hands. I thought I had made her cry.

Instead, she sat up straight and said, "Your grand-mother will be fine. She's always been fine and fully capable of taking care of herself." She stood and tight-ened the belt on her robe.

"You're not even going to *try*?" I said, shocked. "All we have to do is to figure out why Willy is trapped and free him, and they'll let Halmeoni go."

It sounded simple to *say* it, but I quickly realized that actually *doing* it was something else completely.

"Did they say that?" she asked.

"No, but . . . why would they keep her otherwise?" I asked hopefully.

"Because they're *pirates*, Stephen. Amoral, murderous, dangerous men. You cannot trust men like that, dead or alive. And that's the kind of *pirate* you've been aspiring to become? Really!" she said, disgusted.

Now I was furious. "Piventurate! Not pirate!"

"It's not a word," she said bitterly.

It took everything I had to ignore her comment.

"Aren't we going to *do* anything?"

"She's quite cunning when she wants to be. She'll escape. Eventually."

Mom's indifference stunned me into silence. I thought about Willy. I thought about his cry of Transcendent Affliction. He was a ghost, and yet he was suffering. I saw it and I felt it. I could not let that happen to my own grandmother. They had taken her *freedom*. What kind of an afterlife could you lead if you weren't *free*?

"We just need to think this through. I'm not prepared to do anything right now. And neither will you. Don't get any wild ideas in your head. You're not trained and have no experience. Those spirits are not to be meddled with. I think we got just a glimpse of what they are capable of. Maybe they'll get bored and move on. If you like, I can teach you to block out their voices," Mom offered.

No way. I wanted to listen to everything they had to say. I stared at the floor because I didn't want to look at her.

"Did you hear me? Your grandmother will figure something out on her own. It'll be fine. Let's not over-react. It's time you went to school anyway."

"I heard you," I replied. But I didn't like what she had to say, not one bit.

CHAPTER 22

Mr. Huntington didn't even blink twice at me when we passed each other in the hallway, and he acted as if nothing had happened. Little did he know that my being away from school had changed *everything*.

I knew I couldn't go back in time to before I'd found out I could talk to ghosts and all, but for a second, I remembered my last day of school before I had been so unjustly suspended.

So much had changed. I was *different* now. But different was complicated. Different was a double-edged sword.

With Willy and his loyal but menacing crew, not to mention a trapped grandmother — I had too much going on. Funny to think that just a few hours ago, I had been looking forward to school, because now being here put me in a foul mood for no good reason.

"Ahoy!" It was James. What an annoying troll. "Stephen Uh-Oh! Where's your pirate scarf?" Of course, he circled his hands up to his eyes to make two *O*'s.

"Shut up," I told him. I wasn't about to tell him that I was banned from wearing it.

"Heard you got in *trouble*," he continued.

"Want me to knock your teeth out too?" I asked. Today, I had no patience for his mocking tone.

He looked surprised since I usually just ignored him.

"Okay, okay." He put his hands up in surrender and backed away.

That's right, you rascal, walk away.

I shoved my way into the class. When I saw Isabel approaching, I could tell there wasn't enough room in the cloakroom for both of us to pass comfortably. I told her, "Move."

"Rude," she said as she stepped aside.

Ms. Atwal smiled as I emerged from the cloakroom. "Welcome back, Stephen," she said. I was grateful nobody else mentioned the absence of my red bandanna. I wasn't sure if any of them had seen my hair in years.

I returned a smile half-heartedly, glancing up at the clock. The bell was going to ring any second now, so I looked at the doorway, expecting Brandon. He hustled in right before the bell sounded and lunged to his desk.

"Yes!" He did a fist pump. How did he do it? How could he be late, yet never actually *late*?

Shaking my head and laughing at the same time, I waved at him.

Ms. Atwal got our attention by calling, "All right, everybody! Before we start our Mindful Minute, I'm excited to tell you that today we're starting a Social Studies unit."

There was some general grumbling from the class.

"Of course, this area was occupied by Indigenous people first, and we'll start our unit there. After that, we'll talk about European settlement. Anybody know the funny nickname of the captain of the ship who got shipwrecked here?" She looked around the class.

Why, *why* were we talking about *him* at school? I suppressed a groan.

"*You know who it is, don't you, lad?*" a frosty voice I knew well whispered.

Sliced Cheek sat with his legs crossed in the empty seat next to me before he disappeared.

Brandon and I ate our lunches outside in our usual spot near the woods. We'd had a fire drill during recess — was there no end to Mr. Huntington's cruelty? — and hadn't had a chance to talk privately all morning. Do you know how hard it was to keep my cool during class when I was visited by Sliced Cheek and not say anything about it for *hours*? And the award for Best Rookie Baksu goes to *me*.

Brandon didn't know about the little visit from Sliced Cheek, the kkwaenggwari, or Halmeoni being trapped. I almost didn't know how to begin.

"Bro, where's your bandanna?" Brandon asked.

"Mr. Huntington told me to leave it at home." I ran my fingers through my hair. It was a feeling I still wasn't used to.

"Boo. Why is he infringing on your personal style?"

"Because he can," I huffed.

"I hate authority." Brandon shook his head in disgust.

"My bandanna wasn't hurting *anybody*. People who have power shouldn't just throw their weight around because they can." I paused, gathering my thoughts. "They should use it to help other people!" My words lingered in my head.

Brandon nodded in agreement.

I took a vicious bite of my cucumber and cheese sandwich.

"When is my mother going to realize that I'm twelve and I need more food than this 'light lunch' nonsense?" I chewed angrily. "I'm basically *always* hungry!"

Brandon looked embarrassed. His bento box lunch was bursting with small tortillas, guacamole, and a good, heaping portion of diced chicken.

We both ate in silence. I was done eating before Brandon, and while I zipped up my lunch box, he quietly handed me a folded tortilla, generously filled. I gratefully took it.

He bumped my tortilla gently with his, and we both proceeded to shove them into our mouths in one large greedy bite. Neither of us could close our mouths, so we sprayed bits of chicken around laughing.

After I calmed down and managed to swallow, I said, "So, I've got something to tell you."

Brandon suddenly looked focused. "What's wrong?"

"Something happened this morning. Well, actually a bunch of things happened."

He raised his eyebrows.

"Are you ready for a long story?"

"Is it a *ghost* story?" he asked, intrigued.

"Unfortunately, that's the only kind I have right now." I began to tell him everything.

"What do you think I should do?" I asked. "Do you think I have to go back? I mean, I think I have to go back, right?"

"Bro, it's your *grandmother*. Is this even a question?" he asked. "You're a baksu, right? No changing that."

"But my mother said . . ."

"Listen, your mother's a smart lady. Nobody doubts that. But even smart people are *wrong*. Like that person from *Collins English Dictionary* who emailed me back yesterday and said, 'Piventurate, while clever, does not meet the standards of a new word to be included in this year's edition, as it is not commonly used.' What do they know about it? *Pfft!* And what does your mother know too?" Brandon was speaking with a lot of pent-up passion today.

I snickered. At least he got an answer from a dictionary editor; I had heard crickets. "Yeah, what does she know, anyway? Besides, I think she's lost all of her powers."

"As far as I'm concerned, it's settled. Isn't this what it's all about, having more piventurate experiences?"

I nodded again. That was what I'd thought it was all about when my biggest problem was finding a stick to play with. I had way bigger problems now.

"So, what would a piventurate who could talk to ghosts do?" Brandon asked.

"Go back to The Midway," I replied quietly. "I should help Willy — if I can. I should try. By helping Willy, I'll help my grandmother."

"Exactly. Now you're thinking like a piventurate with extra skills. I would. If *I* could." Brandon looked wistful. "That would be an awesome adventure."

Extra skills? I guess I hadn't thought of it like that. I hadn't earned them. I mean, I didn't know if seeing ghosts was a *skill* exactly, but maybe that wasn't the point. Brandon made it seem so black-and-white. But what he didn't know was that there was a whole lot of gray. Gray ghosts, mostly.

He stared at me intently for a few moments. "I can see you waffling."

Brandon knew me too well.

"What's the problem?" he asked.

"*What's the problem?*" I cried back. "Dude, I'm *scared.* I'm not like you!"

"What does *that* mean?" He looked offended.

I think I was letting my exhaustion get the better of me. This was not supposed to turn into a fight with my best friend.

"You're . . . fearless," I told him. "Me? I just *want* to be fearless." My entire body wilted.

"I think you know what I'm going to say next," Brandon warned. "My new favorite expression."

"*Are we complaining or are we training?*" we said together. I was too tired to laugh.

"That doesn't help," I said. Then I let out a huge cry of frustration. "This sucks!"

My angst left even Brandon silent.

"I'm not even supposed to *be* in The Midway. Remember? Disappearing body parts! Mom said being there was a *mistake.* Second: Evil Pirate Crew! Third:

No idea what I'm doing! I don't know why he's stuck!"
I was pacing. "Even if I go back, and I'm not saying I'm
going back, what do I *do*? How can I possibly make a
decision like this?"

"What if you left it up to the universe to make your
decision for you? The ultimate test of fate?" he asked calmly.

"What do you mean? You're kind of starting to creep
me out with all this mystical talk."

"Blame my mother." He paused briefly. "It all boils
down to rock, paper, scissors."

"What?" I stared at him in disbelief.

"Rock, paper, scissors," he repeated. "The ultimate
game of chance. And destiny."

"You want me to leave all my decisions up to a game
of rock, paper, scissors?" A faint memory of Mom playing with me as a little kid crept into my mind, but she
called it by the Korean name: kawi, bawi, bo.

"It's perfect — think about it. If you win, you were
meant to win. In a cosmic-fate sense. If you lose, the universe wanted you to lose. Either way, it's out of your hands!"

"I don't know," I said, unconvinced.

"Let's try it," he suggested as he held out his fist.

I frowned for a second. Really? Was this the best way
to make a decision? Brandon did have a point, though.

Win or lose, it wasn't up to me, was it? It felt almost freeing to not have to make a decision, and to know the decision was already made by a more powerful force. Fate.

I stuck out my hand. "On three."

"Wait!" Brandon stopped me. "You must clearly state what you're betting on!"

I sighed. Geez, when did he get so dramatic?

"Okay, okay." I gathered my thoughts. "So, let's say I win this game of rock, paper, scissors. That means I will return to The Midway to help William J. Sapperton so that he may be free and not be relegated to The Chasm . . . and when I do so, his dastardly crew will then free the spirit of my dead grandmother from her current position as a captive in a brig."

"Well, it just sounds weird when you say it like that," Brandon muttered.

"Let me add, not exactly sure what I'm supposed to *do* in order to make this all happen, but whatever, let's let fate decide!" I held out my fist. "Let's go already!"

"One, two, three!" we both said, gently pumping our fists in time to our counting.

On three, Brandon showed scissors and I showed rock.

"It's done," he smirked.

"You lost on purpose!"

"Come on! How did I know what you were going to play?" Brandon said with exaggerated outrage. "As if you weren't going to play rock," he mumbled quietly.

I pouted at him. How did *he* know?

"It was fate, then," I admitted, more as a question than a statement.

"Finally! You're getting it!" He slapped my shoulder. He'd been slapping me a lot lately.

"What are you doing tomorrow?" I asked.

"That depends. What are *you* doing?" he replied mischievously.

"I'm not sure exactly. I'll figure it out."

Fate had spoken. I was supposed to help Willy and Halmeoni. I wished fate had given me a step-by-step handbook with instructions and very detailed illustrations.

"Aye. I know you will." Brandon smiled as he snapped on his eyepatch and picked up the twig sitting next to him. "Lunch is almost over. Are you ready for some gentle — *very gentle* — swordplay?"

"Aye. We're training. No more complaining." I snapped my eyepatch on and prepared myself.

CHAPTER 23

Mom was sitting at the kitchen table with her laptop open and a stack of papers next to it. Highly engrossed in reading. Excellent. I went to the kitchen, filled up a water bottle, and grabbed a bag of sweet potato snacks. I gave it a shake. Not filling enough. I also picked up a few granola bars. Quietly, I placed the food in my backpack next to both of the kkwaenggwari, which I had wrapped up in towels so they wouldn't clang around.

"I'm meeting Brandon for a bike ride today, okay?" I told Mom.

She looked up briefly before she said, "Sure." Her eyes went back to the screen.

Maybe Mom didn't notice the large dark bags under my eyes, or at least she didn't say anything about them, but I sure noticed hers. I hadn't slept in two days. Literally zero winks. I didn't know if she hadn't slept at all like me, but she looked exhausted too.

The first sleepless night, I couldn't relax because every time I closed my eyes, I imagined Sliced Cheek staring back at me. But last night, it was because I kept hearing things. I had taken the kkwaenggwari from Mom's closet yesterday and left them on my night table. I had lots of room now that the remnants of my copy of *Treasure Island* were stuffed into a drawer.

All night, I could feel something. The gongs weren't exactly *talking* to me with words like, *Hey, Stephen, how are you?* No, it wasn't like that. It was different. There was an energy coming from the surface of the brass, a hum I could not define. Just looking at them, I knew that I had won that game of rock, paper, scissors for a reason.

When I picked up one of the kkwaenggwari in the middle of the night, my fingers buzzed, like the wings of a fly gently dancing across my skin.

Go-between. Listener. Helper.

I had no choice but to do exactly the opposite of what my mother had told me. I wasn't disobeying her. I was following the path the universe had laid out for me.

Halmeoni needed help. Mom wasn't going to even *try*. Talk about the world's worst daughter.

Willy needed help too, but for totally different reasons. Yesterday, I didn't really know where to start. But the more I thought about how I was going to help him, the more I thought about one thing he had said: *When you lose your way, you need to go back to the beginning.*

And in the very beginning of all of this, there was his display at the museum. That's where I was going to start.

"I'll be back later!" I yelled down the hallway as I slipped into my Crocs. My bandanna may have been banned from school, but it wasn't banned from my weekends, so I put my spare one on.

I focused in on Mom's purse sitting on the hallway table, and I hoped they were still there. My fingers pried open the front pocket. There they were. At least now I wasn't going to have to use any of my allowance. I added the tickets to the rest of my supplies in my backpack and I was ready to go.

When I emerged from the underground parkade, I looked out at the marina. *Blackbeard's Vestige* was still gone. Must be some adventure it was on. In fact, lots of boats were gone today, and the marina had a deserted feel about it. Funny how after a few days of ghost hauntings, I had nearly forgotten about the boat, which only days ago had been so important to me.

The seawall was full of morning joggers and people out walking their dogs. I rode over to the spot where I was meeting Brandon.

While I waited, I sat on an empty bench and tried identifying nautical flags.

There was one boat that had hoisted flags that were just wrong! You couldn't hoist the *Alpha* flag (meaning "Diver down, keep clear") when you were *moored* in a marina. Worse, this boat also flew *Juliet*, which meant there was a fire on board! Some boat owners were not worthy. I shook my head in disgust. Did they even care that there was a well-defined standard international code for these things? If I had a boat, I'd know all my proper flags *and* when to fly them.

I felt my back pocket for my Jolly Roger and remembered how sad it had looked when I shoved it in the crack of the dory. One day, maybe I'd get to raise it on a proper boat, where it would fly proudly off a mast and snap in the wind. Deciding it would be safer in my backpack, I folded it up and tucked it into a small zippered compartment.

"Hey!" Brandon yelled in my ear.

I turned quickly to face him. "What?"

"I called your name, like, five times!" He straddled his bike.

"I didn't hear," I admitted. I was more tired than I'd realized.

He shrugged his shoulders. "Okay, so what's the plan?"

"We ride to the Museum of Cedar Coast. I think we need to start there."

"And?" Brandon asked, waiting for more information.

"I can't really explain it yet. It's just a hunch."

His eyes narrowed, and he seemed unconvinced.

"Sorry, I'm tired. Just trust me," I urged.

His face relaxed and he nodded. "I trust you."

"Let's do this!" I said as I jumped onto my bike and hoped that I was right.

CHAPTER 24

We locked up our bikes in front of the museum, then I noticed Brandon came to a complete stop.

"Wait," he said. "I don't have any money for admission."

I reached into my backpack. "No problem." I smiled smugly before I flashed him the two complimentary tickets Margo had given Mom the last time we were here.

"Awesome!" He peered into the bag. "Oh, you brought snacks too. Cool. You're prepared today."

I was feeling pretty good about how things were going. I *was* prepared today. Also delirious, but what else would you expect when you hadn't slept in two days?

The fresh air danced gently across my face, and I looked at the clouds rolling briskly across the sky. I wanted to close my eyes to feel the breeze, but I was worried I'd fall asleep standing up. The view from Sunrise Beach Park didn't disappoint. As usual, I scanned the water for *The Climb* but could find no trace of Daniela and her boat.

There were lots of other awesome boats scattered across the harbor, though, and next to me was my best friend. I didn't know what was going to happen, but I did know that it felt piventurate-y.

"We've got to play it cool," I reminded Brandon as we walked up to the entrance doors.

"I've got this," he assured me.

"Try not to use that special new smile of yours."

Brandon feigned shock. "What's wrong with my smile?" He, of course, smiled.

"It's weird, stop it."

"Okay, okay."

Before entering, Brandon and I gave each other side-eyes and grinned.

We walked up to the ticket counter, and I was very glad to see that it was not the same person who was there when I'd come with Mom.

"Good morning," the woman at the counter said.

"Are we first?" Brandon said loudly.

I wanted to smack him.

"I'm super excited to see this museum!" Brandon said stiffly, flashing too many teeth.

I elbowed him in the ribs.

"Can we use these vouchers?" I asked calmly, placing the tickets down on the counter. One of us had better act normal, and it was obvious Brandon wasn't capable of it.

"Sure!" the woman replied as she settled into her chair. She pulled the tickets toward her. "Do you need a map?"

"Yes, please." Totally a lie. I knew exactly where I was going.

"Here you go. Enjoy the displays."

Leisurely, I reached for the map. Brandon started a quick gallop toward the exhibits, but I grabbed his elbow and held him back.

"What happened to playing it cool?" I hissed.

"I'm trying! Hey, you've had lots of adventures recently. It's my first one! I guess I'm excited," Brandon explained. He closed his eyes and told himself, "Find your center." He held both palms facedown in front of his stomach and pushed them down slowly.

I watched him blankly. "Are you done?"

He puffed out a short breath and nodded.

"It's through here." I guided Brandon through the displays.

"Okay, so what exactly are we doing here?" he whispered.

"I'm back at the beginning."

"Right, reconnecting with Willy. Good place to start."

The exhibit was just as I remembered. Everything from the first time I'd been here earlier in the week looked the same, but everything was so different. Especially me.

We paused in front of Willy's wax statue. We both considered it for several seconds.

"Isn't it obvious that he's a pirate?" Brandon asked, reading the title of the display. "Just a 'shipwrecked merchant,' as if!"

"I know," I agreed.

"Did he actually look like this?"

"Less waxy. More ghostly."

Brandon rolled his eyes.

We took a few steps and then stopped in front of the pedestal that held Willy's sea chest. This was the beginning. Now what?

"Is this the box that you touched, creating a special multidimensional bond between you and Willy?" Brandon asked.

"Yup."

"Is a sea chest the same as a *treasure chest*?" Brandon looked at me for verification.

"Seems like it, right?"

"Oh sure, I have a *treasure chest*, but I'm just a regular merchant sailor," Brandon said sarcastically.

Willy's box — now that we were right in front of it — drew me closer, like a magnet.

I was lost in thought, staring at the box, when something occurred to me.

"The nameplate is still missing," I told Brandon.

"Nameplate? What do you mean?"

"Oh, I forgot to tell you this part." I felt sheepish.

He turned to face me.

"Last time, I did touch the box, but it was mostly the nameplate on the front. See that small patch, under the keyhole? That's where it was. It must have been loose because it fell off and landed on the ground. Then my mom kind of . . . kicked it away." I shrugged awkwardly.

Brandon looked at me quizzically. "Your mom kicked the nameplate? That's just weird. Why didn't she say something to the staff?" Brandon crossed his arms and stared at the box.

"It *was* weird. But she said she didn't want it known that I was a 'desecrator of local artifacts.'" I used air quotes.

Brandon held back a snort. "Wow. She talks funny."

"I know."

"Okay, so what's it look like?" Brandon asked. "Do you think it's still around here?"

"It's about the size of a business card. The brass is tarnished," I said.

Then I froze.

The word "brass" suddenly appeared to me like a big blinking neon sign. The nameplate was *brass*. The kkwa-enggwari were brass. Mom said brass gives the courage to see the truth.

"Oh my," I murmured. "It's exactly what Willy needs."

The staticky conversation of people speaking over a two-way radio pricked my ears.

"Pretend you're reading!" I said as a security guard doing his patrol passed us. I made sure we looked like totally normal twelve-year-old boys enjoying a museum. The guard nodded and kept walking.

Once I was sure that he was gone, a feeling of urgency overwhelmed me. I crouched and started scanning the floor.

"Bro, what are you doing?" Brandon asked.

"The nameplate. I *have* to find the nameplate," I said, trying to keep my emotions in check. "I thought it went under the dress." I pointed to the display next to the stand where the sea chest was exhibited. I was practically on my stomach now. Brandon joined me on the ground.

I finally saw it. The brass was dull, but at just the right angle, I could see it reflect the smallest sliver of light.

"There it is!" I said excitedly. The full skirt of the costume on the mannequin had sheltered the nameplate well enough that none of the staff had seen it in the few days since it had fallen off.

"Doesn't anybody vacuum around here?" Brandon dusted his hands.

Before I could answer, before I could even think, I lunged for it. Maybe I was delirious from lack of sleep, maybe I had a moment of fearlessness, or maybe I was just dense, but Willy's brass nameplate was now in my hands.

It should have felt cold — the air-conditioning was blasting in the museum — but it didn't. It felt warm, like it was gently humming in my hands. There was the renewed feeling of a jolt of energy surging through my arm, just like last time.

As soon as I held it, I knew I wasn't just supposed to find it. I was supposed to take it to Willy. I knew because it was telling me so.

"Are you okay, boys?" The guard! He was back.

Brandon popped up like a spring-loaded toy, while I stayed down on my hands and knees longer than I probably should have.

"Oh, we're fine! Everything's fine!" Brandon said with a little too much enthusiasm.

With the grace and ease of a wave gently coming ashore, I turned around and put my hand to the back of my head to tuck the brass nameplate into my bandanna, all while standing up.

"I just thought I . . ." My mind spun furiously. "I think I saw a . . . mouse," I said with a look of shock and disgust.

The guard, in his yellow and black uniform, reached for the radio on his belt. "Maintenance!" he yelled into the microphone. He turned back to us and said, "Thanks for spotting that. It would be a real shame for these artifacts to be ruined."

"We'll just be on our way, then!" Brandon said loudly.

We grabbed each other's arms and started walking quickly, but not too quickly, through the rest of the museum. The brass plate felt like it was going to slip, so I tightened the knot at the base of my skull to make sure it didn't slide out. Turned out the bandanna wasn't just a statement piece. It was useful!

"Is that it? Is that what you wanted to do here?" he asked through clenched teeth. "Nothing else?"

I had never been so sure of anything in my life.

"Yes, this is it." I closed my eyes and exhaled. I reached behind my head to touch the plate through the fabric of the bandanna. "I have what I need. I have what Willy needs."

The staticky sound of the guard's radio shut us up. Brandon had his lips puckered up, like he was desperate to say something more but trying very hard to keep it in. It seemed to take *forever* to finish walking through all the galleries. When we finally went through the gift shop and exited the building, he exploded.

"Oh my pirates!" Brandon grabbed the sides of his head, and his eyes were bursting wide. "That was amazing! *You* were amazing!" He grabbed me by the upper arms and started jumping up and down. "*I think I saw a mouse!*" he imitated me. "It was genius!"

The blood rushed to my face instantly with his compliment.

"Thanks for helping me." I held out a closed fist.

He bumped my fist in return and said, "I think that counts as our first real adventure together, don't you?"

"That totally counts," I agreed. "It's definitely not our last."

I slipped my bandanna off to retrieve the nameplate and held it in my hand as my thumb gently traced over the name: *William J. Sapperton.* The edges of the individual letters were slightly raised. The rest of the plate was mostly smooth, except for the thin strip of space just above where Willy's name was etched.

That section felt grainy and just the tiniest bit rough. I flicked it in my hand so that it would catch the light and I could get a better look.

When I held the plate at just the right angle, I could see the faint shadow of a word that was mostly removed. It was the word *Captain.*

"What is it?" Brandon asked.

"Look here." I showed him. "Do you see it?"

"Captain." Brandon looked up. "Why would that be rubbed out? I'd love to be a captain!"

I inhaled deeply. "It's so strange! He kept telling me to just call him Willy."

"Maybe you can get some answers when you see him again."

I held the brass plate tightly in my hand. "With this, maybe he can see what he needs to see. I'm going to give Willy a piece of his past."

"I just got goosies from you saying that!" He showed me his forearm.

I forced myself to smile, and I wished I could feel as excited as he was, but something about the nameplate troubled me.

Brandon stopped in his tracks and grabbed my elbow. "Wait. We just *stole* something."

He was right. We had just *stolen* from a museum. But instead of worrying about getting arrested, I chuckled. "Maybe we're more pirate-y than we thought."

"Nah, we're still more piventurate-y."

"Plus, we're just returning an item to its original owner," I reminded him. "That's not stealing at all."

"That's why it's important that those stubborn dictionary editors recognize *piventurate* as a legitimate word!" Brandon said. "Pretty soon, I'm just going to start calling their offices — forget email!"

I agreed completely.

We walked back to the bike rack. Before slipping it into my backpack, next to the kkwaenggwari and my Jolly Roger, I gave the nameplate one final look.

Then I glanced at my watch. It was almost eleven o'clock, so I still had an hour to get there. After the high of successfully accomplishing our mission, the adrenaline rush was wearing off and I struggled with my bicycle lock.

My lack of sleep was really getting to me now.

Still unable to get my lock undone, I closed my eyes. It was as though I could have fallen asleep right on the spot. Then I heard it. The faintest of sounds at first, but like trying to focus my eyes on a blurry object, I started to focus my *ears*. I could hear the dimmest of cries. It startled me to realize that I knew who it was. The sound of Willy's Transcendent Affliction could not be mistaken.

I glanced toward Rail's End.

"*Get a move on, boy.*" The large ghost with the skull and crossbones tattoos on his face hovered right before me. He was alone, and maybe I should have been thankful for that, but in a strange way, I suddenly missed Sliced Cheek. This guy may have not had an open flesh wound, but he was twice the size of Sliced Cheek and, in his own way, twice as scary.

I somehow managed to spit out, "I know, I know. I have a plan now."

"Hurry. Time's running out."

"Uh, Stephen?" Brandon asked. "Why are you talking to yourself?"

"I'm not."

The tattooed ghost floated next to Brandon and smirked. *"So, this is your best mate?"*

I nodded slightly.

"I've seen his family. His mother is with child. But you seem like you're sufficiently motivated now, so I guess we don't need to do what we had planned . . ." he said ominously.

"Uh, is there a ghost standing next to me?" Brandon asked, looking worried. He scratched at his shoulder as if he had felt the frigid touch of the spirit beside him.

The tattooed ghost cackled and disappeared.

CHAPTER 25

"**W**hat's going on?" Brandon asked. He looked over his shoulder a few times.

"Somebody was here, but they're gone now," I whispered. I sure wasn't sleepy anymore! Sliced Cheek and his crew sure were talented in motivating a reluctant baksu!

"You know, I think I *felt* something!" Instead of being petrified, he actually seemed *excited* about it. "Are you sure you don't want me to come with you?" Brandon asked again. "I might be able to help!"

"You've already helped," I told him, trying to shake off the surprise of seeing the tattooed ghost alone. I inhaled a big breath of air. "But I think I've got to go on my own."

The Midway wasn't for the living. I knew this to be a fact. I'd mistakenly ended up there once; everybody's allowed to make a mistake once in a while. But this time, I was *deliberately* going back to The Midway. I knew there was no chickening out now, but there was a fine line between brave and bananas. I was still not sure which side of the line I was on yet.

We stood at the intersection of Hemlock and Shipyard streets. One way led Brandon back to his house. The other way led me to Rail's End.

Brandon tried to hide his disappointment, but I knew him too well. "Okay, I guess I'll head home then," he said, resigned.

"I know this sucks. I know you want to come with me. I wish you could."

"I get it. I'm no baksu." He looked away.

"Haven't you noticed? I don't really have a clue what I'm doing! You helped me sort everything out. I might be a baksu, but a baksu is nothing without friends, dead or alive, to help him."

I tried to catch his eyes with mine. He finally looked at me.

"I'll tell you everything. I promise I won't leave out a single detail."

"You'd better not." He hopped on his bike and glanced at his watch. "It's getting late. You should get going."

"I'll see you tomorrow . . . I guess?"

"Did you tell your mom you were going?" Brandon asked, just as he was about to pedal away.

My face dropped. She had looked so exhausted this morning, she was probably asleep at her desk anyway. "She'll figure it out. I hope."

I locked up my bike but fully expected it to be gone when I got back the next day. Rail's End was that kind of neighborhood. The crowd around the steam clock had started to gather, and I knew I didn't have too much time left.

From a block away, the road stood a little higher, and it was easy to get a good view of the clock. It was funny to think that all the people gathered around it just came to watch a clock spurt out some steam — what they didn't know was that the best part of the steam clock was what was *underneath* and *beyond*.

But I was still nervous as heck! Even though I knew how to get there, I also knew that I wasn't supposed to *be* there. Every step closer to the clock caused my heart to beat more violently in my chest. The sweat on my palms was building at an alarming rate. Wiping my hands down on my pants had no effect. I approached the steam clock carefully but quickly. Peeking up at the hands on the clockface, I realized I had only a few minutes left.

After weaving my way through the crowd, I found a good spot close to the base of the clock, almost exactly where I had stood before. I wanted to repeat everything precisely as I had done the first time. Mom said it was the combination of the noon sun, the steam from the clock, and the location itself. Everything had to be just right. I closed my eyes and started to breathe slowly and deliberately. *Universe, don't let me down now*, I thought.

When the first of the twelve whistles sounded, I didn't even flinch. My eyes were still closed, and I let the sound fill my ears. By the fifth whistle, I could feel the cloud of steam was just starting to build. By the tenth whistle, I opened my eyes to look down at my hands. Were they disappearing, or were they obscured by the mist? A small wave of panic started to build, and I worked hard to push it away.

There was something else I hadn't noticed the first time I was here. The inner workings of the clock, behind the glass. *Brass.* The pipes at the top of the clock. Also brass. The body of the clock was black, but maybe that was just paint. I reached out with my finger to test my theory. Yup, I could feel the energy pulsating off the clock. It was brass too. I placed my entire hand on the side of the clock to feel its strength. I felt electric. More alive than I had ever felt.

By the eleventh whistle, I looked around at the people surrounding me. The cloud was starting to roll out and encompass more and more people, me included. As my eyes danced around the faces, through a break in the steam, I saw the face of my *mother.* The sight of her threw me. What was she doing here? On the twelfth whistle, when the steam clock unleashed its most powerful whistle and the largest burst of mist, she lunged. She made a grab for my free hand, and with her other hand, she touched the clock.

CHAPTER 26

I wasn't exactly *experienced* at traveling to The Midway, but I knew from last time that it takes several seconds to get reoriented. When my senses started to come into focus, I heard a booming voice shout, "You!"

There was Willy, looking as faded and washed out as he had when I last saw him. He raced up to me and, because he sounded so annoyed, I braced myself for a tirade. But instead, he flew right past me. He stopped to hover in front of Mom. Immediately, he began to wag a finger at her.

"I'd recognize this face anywhere! You liar! You made me a promise!" His words were filled with rage and his body flickered in and out.

Looking very calm, despite the angry ghost inches from her face, she said, "Yes, it has been twenty years." She cocked her head to the side. "But if you will recall, I never said exactly *when* I'd be back. And look. Here I am. I fulfilled my promise!"

Then something astonishing happened. My mother laughed. Not just a chuckle or a smirk either. A full-body laugh — the kind of laugh that makes every muscle ache and tears stream down your face. It was the strangest thing I had ever seen. Willy, too, was taken aback and glanced over at me quizzically.

"Wait," he said slowly as he focused on me. "Are you her *son*?"

I nodded and found myself scratching my head through my bandanna.

"Well, I'll be." Willy paced back and forth while he cautiously regarded the two of us.

Mom had begun to recover her senses but held her arms across her sore belly. "My goodness, I haven't laughed like that . . ."

"Ever," I interrupted.

"I fail to see the humor in all of this," Willy replied.

"Mom, you two know each other?" I was still

puzzled by what was happening.

"She was the trickster who told me she'd help me. She said, '*Oh I'll come back, Willy! I know things,*'" he mocked her voice.

Mom's good mood faded, and she turned up her nose. "I *did* ask around, but I couldn't quite figure out why you were trapped. Not even the really ancient spirits had any insight into your situation. I admit, I eventually forgot about it."

Willy let out a little whimper. "Never trust the living. You just forgot about me like a piece of old garbage."

"You needn't take it personally. I've tried to avoid all ghosts, not just you."

I nodded. That part was true.

"Don't take it *personally*? You, woman, are colder than a slab of Atlantic cod." Willy spoke with enough venom to knock out an elephant. "Why have you returned, then?" His eyes darkened.

"I have, intentionally, kept away from the steam clock for many years, and I only returned to help my son." She turned to me.

"You have *got* to stop keeping secrets from me!" I yelled.

"You're one to talk." She scoffed. "You didn't exactly mention where you and Brandon were heading off to this morning, did you?"

"How did you know I'd be here?" I felt a little contrite.

"Mudang, remember?" she said, pointing at herself. "Even if I'm not what I once was, or could have been, I'm not completely powerless. And some ghosts are really terrible gossips. I simply chose not to ignore all the chattering this morning."

"They're talking about me?" I asked, looking around suspiciously.

"They've not much else to do, have they, Stephen?"

That unsettled feeling you get when you realize people have been discussing you behind your back rushed over me.

"So what is it, then? Why have you two returned?" Willy seemed more annoyed than angry now.

I summoned some strength to speak. "Willy, by any chance have you recently spoken to members of your former crew?"

He glared at me. "What concern do you have for my crew?"

Mom and I glanced at each other.

"Well, they ..." I stumbled. What an awkward thing to tell him. *Hey, Willy, your crew kidnapped my grandmother, so I'm forced to help you.*

Willy looked confused and eventually lost his patience. "They what?"

"They, um ..."

"Boy, there are few things my crew can do that will be of any surprise. Just spit out the words."

"They've captured the spirit of my grandmother," I finally said.

"What kind of nonsense is this?" Willy exclaimed. "Was she stuck ... like me?"

I shook my head.

"She was a free spirit?"

I nodded.

"But now they've *trapped* her?" His eyes widened.

"In the brig of a ship, apparently."

"For what purpose?" He continued to grill me.

"To encourage me to come back here to figure out a way to free *you*."

"It's a form of emotional blackmail," Mom said flatly.

Willy hovered in the air and stared off into the distance. Then he shuddered and covered his face with his hands. "I don't deserve their loyalty. Not after the way I treated them at the end," he sobbed.

"They said you were an excellent captain."

"*Captain*," he howled. "So loyal. Even in the afterlife. My crew are simply the best of men."

I sure hoped this bout of crying wasn't going to lead to *that sound* again.

"They want to see you free, and back to your old self," I said. "There's not much time."

"Their motivation is unimportant. It's still a kind of blackmail," Mom whispered to me. "Pirates," she muttered loudly, shaking her head disapprovingly.

Willy regained his composure and gave Mom a long stare. He sniffled before clearing his throat. "No matter. As you can see, it's almost over." He looked down at his fading body. "What can you do now that I haven't already tried over and over?"

"There is one thing you've never tried." Getting ready to continue, I faltered.

I inhaled deeply while I scanned The Midway. Everything was familiar. The dappled light of the midday sun filtered down into the cavern. Above, the fuzzy images of people walking and cars driving on the road next to the steam clock. Lifting my hand to look at it, I made sure

I wasn't starting to disappear like last time. I wasn't —
not yet, anyway. But my time here was short, I knew that.

Finally, I blurted out, "I have something that I think
is important."

"Just tell me. I don't want to spend my last moments
in The Midway playing games," Willy said with very
little energy.

"Your nameplate. I have it." It felt like a brick in my
backpack.

"Eh? What's that?"

"Your nameplate!" I said more clearly. "I have it."

"Nameplate?"

"From your sea chest. The one you had on your ship
when you first came here?"

"My old sea chest?" he asked deliberately, sounding
confused.

"I thought . . . maybe you needed it. It's brass."
I looked over at Mom. "And brass . . ."

"Gives courage," she said breathlessly, her eyes wide.

"Courage!" Willy sounded offended. His eyes turned
darker again. "I never lacked courage in my life! How
dare you." He turned up his nose and crossed his arms.

"Do you see why I wanted nothing to do with him?"
Mom leaned in to whisper.

"Where's your courage *now*? Are you just going to let it happen to you? Being cast off into The Chasm? Aren't you going to fight?" I chided. Almost immediately, I regretted my harsh tone.

He needed to see it. I reached into my backpack and retrieved the nameplate. It felt warm in my hands and it thrummed gently. As I held it out for Willy, the plate seemed to shimmer briefly.

"Why is the word *Captain* rubbed out?"

Willy would not look at me.

"He rubbed out his title?" Mom looked at the small piece of brass.

"Do you remember this?" I asked Willy, my arm extended. "Your sea chest. With your name. Your full name and your *title*."

Cautiously, he flew closer to me. A look of thoughtful concentration settled over his face as he focused on the brass plate.

"My old sea chest," Willy breathed. "I had forgotten about it completely."

"How could you forget about such a thing?"

He pursed his lips. "I wanted to forget."

"Forget? Why?" I asked.

While he continued to stare at the small piece of

brass in my hand, his face seemed to soften.

"The box was part of my past. A past I ... wanted to and hoped to walk away from." Timidly, he looked at me. When our eyes met, I suddenly understood. He was ashamed of his past. Ashamed of the things he'd done. Ashamed of having been a pirate.

I swallowed hard before I spoke. "I've always thought pirates were misunderstood."

"Now, now, those were *rumors*. I never said I was a pirate." Willy looked away.

I chose my next words carefully. "Maybe that's the problem. You need to say it. If you don't say it, it's like pretending to be somebody you're not."

Still, Willy refused to meet my eyes.

I tried a different approach. "What if you thought of yourself not as a traditional pirate, but as a piventurate? You were a bold explorer, thirsting for adventure, on the hunt for personal challenges. That kind of idea."

Mom sighed and rolled her eyes.

"Oh, that silly word you told me about before?" Willy asked.

"It's *not* silly!" I snapped. This old ghost was starting to annoy me. "You know how sometimes people hear something and are just super judgey and they jump to conclusions? Some words, like *pirate*, do that to you. Sometimes that's why you need *new* words. Better words! More accurate words."

"Like piventurate?" Mom's voice had a sarcastic edge to it that I did not appreciate.

"Exactly like piventurate!" I declared. "Like it or not, Mom, you know language evolves!"

"Piventurate." Willy said the word carefully. "So, rather like a bold voyager more than anything?"

"Yup. You take the best part of pirates — the courage, the audaciousness — and combine them with a longing for adventure, but with no serious crimes. *Boom!* Piventurate."

"Yes, yes!" Willy said with a sudden burst of enthusiasm. "Your modern interpretation, upon further reflection, is quite beguiling and wholly alluring."

I thought Mom would be disappointed that I didn't understand what the word *beguiling* meant, so I just went with it and didn't ask for clarification.

"You are *Captain* William J. Sapperton. Your ship, *The Eidolon*, landed off the shores of Cedar Coast. Or got shipwrecked, whatever you want to call it. Your past is your past. It's part of you, but so what? Don't let one word with so much baggage define you. Or limit you."

Willy started to reach out his hand, but it trembled and he hesitated.

"*Captain* Sapperton, go on, take it," I urged. I wished he'd hurry, because my arm was getting tired. "Take it. Remember your name, remember everything. Even the stuff that you'd rather forget. You can't just forget it. It's part of you. Then you've got to *accept* it."

"I . . ." Willy was at a loss for words.

"'Good men must die, but death cannot kill their names,'" Mom said faintly.

As usual, Mom continued to baffle me. I turned to look at her.

"It's an old Danish proverb," she explained. She took a step toward Willy. "Take it. You need to."

"What if it doesn't work?" he asked.

"What if it *does*?" I replied.

A frown, which was probably a look of fear more than anything else, came over Willy's face. If I had been stuck in The Midway for one hundred years, I would be a little nervous and scared too.

"Abigail said that spirits can hold onto things if they *really* want to. It has to be important to you. And what's more important than your *name*? Your full name. And your title. Captain William J. Sapperton of *The Eidolon*." I moved my hand closer to him. "To help you remember."

Willy studied my hand. The brass shone faintly. I could feel the nameplate vibrating on my palm. It was calling to Willy.

I continued, "Don't you long for another adventure?"

"Aye," he replied. "That I do."

"Passing from The Midway to The Great Sea would be a good place to start," I told him. "It's time."

Captain Willy J. Sapperton, better known in these parts as Windy Willy, finally extended his arm toward me and reached for his name.

CHAPTER 27

Mom stepped next to me and placed her arm around my shoulders.

"Do you feel that?" she whispered.

The air in The Midway churned around my ankles.

We watched Willy hold the plate tenderly in his left hand. He ran the tip of his right index finger over his engraved name, tracing each letter slowly.

"Thank you, young Stephen." Willy looked up at me. "Having this in my hand, well." He let out a sigh. "I can remember clearly now. Everything. The adventures, the journeys. All of it. The good things and the things that, well, perhaps I'm not entirely proud of. All together. They made me the man I was. The man I am."

Captain Sapperton's ghost began to take on a more defined shape. His spirit started to twinkle as though memories of his pirate days were bringing him back to life, so to speak. I gazed at the old ghost fondly.

"If I were standing at the helm of *The Eidolon* once more, I would happily offer you a position aboard my ship."

Now normally, if a captain of a ship had said that to me, I would have been thrilled — wasn't that something I had always wanted? But having already met the rest of Captain Sapperton's crew, I wasn't too keen on joining them. I needed to find myself a less scary crowd.

"But you'd have to start off as a powder monkey," he teased. "Young boys are never given positions of serious responsibility. You could work yourself up to quartermaster, but it could take years."

I wasn't sure what to say at this point.

"And then, just maybe, you could be my first mate," he said.

"It would have been an honor, sir." I saluted, but I doubted Sliced Cheek would have been happy about me taking his job.

"Er…um…" He cleared his throat. "I wanted to apologize for any potentially offensive actions of my crew."

"They were trying to help their captain," I replied. "They knew I needed some motivating. They're very good at their jobs."

Willy jerked his head to the large rock that had separated him from the freedom of The Great Sea.

Five gnarly faces stared back at me. Sliced Cheek gave me a creepy wave with just the tips of his fingers. "Hullo there." He leered at me, leaving me feeling unnerved. Was he incapable of *not* being spooky?

"Hey! Where's my grandmother?" I shouted at Sliced Cheek, suddenly remembering that there was more to this job than making sure Willy didn't disappear into The Chasm.

"She's … nearby," Sliced Cheek said. "You'll see her again. If this works." Then he turned to Willy. "Are you ready, sir?"

"Men, I thank you for sticking by ol' Captain Willy. I lost my way. But I think I'm back, if you'll have me," he said humbly.

The crew started barking and howling. I guess that was their way of saying yes.

"Alls anybody needs is a little *motivation*, ain't that right, Captain?" the ghost with one eye said.

"That's right, Scoop. We all just need a spark to get us going," Captain Sapperton replied as he looked down at the brass nameplate he held in his hands.

He nodded at me before his shoulders heaved slightly — then he turned to face the wall of rock that had trapped him for so long.

"Thank you for reminding me that one should never be ashamed of one's past. The past makes you who you are." He held up his nameplate.

I announced loudly, "I never even mentioned that there's a pancake restaurant named after you! That's pretty impressive, isn't it?"

"It's slightly overpriced," Mom said.

I smacked her arm. What a mood killer she could be.

"Well, I'll be." Willy's chest puffed out so much that if the buttons on his vest had been real, they would have popped. "I suppose it's time for Captain William J. Sapperton to have another adventure! Boys, have you ever heard the term *piventurate*?"

"Come on, Captain. Join us!" the ghost with the tattooed face urged. "We've been waitin' on you for a long time."

"*The Great Sea is the place where we are free*," Sliced Cheek sang. It was the first time Sliced Cheek's voice had not creeped me out. It sounded almost pleasant.

Floating up to the wall, his crewmen nearby, Willy hesitated. In his left hand he still held his nameplate. With his right hand, he reached out to gently touch the surface of the coarse stone. Willy closed his eyes.

"*The Great Sea is the place where we are free.*" His voice warbled, and the song was not nearly as pretty as it had been from Abigail's mouth, or even Sliced Cheek's, but it was a *song*, nonetheless. Willy pushed his hand through the solid rock easily.

My mouth dropped in astonishment and so did his. I grabbed Mom's arm. "It worked!" I shrieked, exhilarated by what I had just seen.

The ghosts whooped and hollered their approval. Captain William J. Sapperton had never looked so thrilled.

"The power of remembering who you really are," Mom said as she watched everything unfold with very little expression on her face. "I should have known."

"The power to help Willy finally leave The Midway?" I asked her.

She nodded. "Looks like it. He just needed a bit more courage to see things clearly. All these years, trapped. All these years hiding his pirate past, denying his true self."

"Remind you of anyone?" I asked.

She glared at me.

I smirked. "I've been telling you all along that the world *needs* the word *piventurate*. All of this could have really been avoided if we had the proper names for things."

"My boy!" Willy said. He pushed his hand back and forth, through the rock and back out again. "I can do it! I can do it!"

He sailed around The Midway, giggling with a kind of childlike glee. Who knew an old ghost could be sort of cute?

Willy eventually stopped his shouting and calmed down enough to say to Mom, "I suppose in a way you did fulfill your promise to me. You're not the worst spirit talker, but certainly not the most punctual."

Mom shrugged her shoulders indifferently.

I turned to Sliced Cheek and the crew. "Okay, this is lovely and all that. I did my part. Now, my grandmother! You must free her."

"Of course, little Stephen. She's right behind us. Come get her," Sliced Cheek said as he vanished through the rock.

"I bid you adieu, for now. Thank you for what you have done for me," Willy told me, his eyes shimmering. There was more definition to his body, and I knew that he was no longer bound for The Chasm. He was bound for a place where he would live out the rest of his afterlife free as a bird.

"I'm a baksu. It's my job." I saluted again. "See you on the other side, then."

Willy tipped his hat and without any further hesitation, he flew through the wall of rock, and the rest of his crew disappeared right behind him.

For the first time in a hundred years, Captain William J. Sapperton left The Midway and passed to The Great Sea.

CHAPTER 28

The Midway was suddenly quiet as Mom and I stood there alone.

"What do you mean, 'See you on the other side'?" Mom asked, breaking the silence.

"Well, we're going to The Great Sea too, aren't we? That's where Halmeoni is! That's where the spirits are supposed to be."

"We're not spirits," Mom reminded me.

"*The Great Sea is the place where we are free.*" When I said the words, they didn't become a song the same way they did when the ghosts said them, but they *felt* good anyway. "I know, I know. I just want you to see it. Once. It's your only chance."

"How exactly are we going to pass through the rather large wall of solid stone?" Mom asked, pointing her finger at it.

"Last time, I needed Abigail." I remembered when she'd brushed my shoulder and touched my head; she was the reason I'd been able to pass through The Nexus. I puckered my lips. I may have had a connection to Willy, but I knew I also had a connection with her. I wished she were here.

"No sign of your little friend, sadly. I guess we'll just wait until the noon whistle tomorrow. I'm sure your grandmother is fine."

"Why do you keep saying that?" I shouted. "You don't know that she's fine! We have to find out for ourselves! Couldn't they at least have brought her to us?"

"Need I remind you?" Mom asked, as she looked for a place to sit.

"I know, I know: *pirates*!" I said, frustrated. "Maybe we need to wait for Abigail to come back. She said she always pops in to check on Willy."

"You did manage to deduce a way to free Captain Sapperton. You should feel pleased," Mom said. Was that a *compliment*?

"Yeah, I guess my idea worked. But what about Halmeoni? She's the reason I did all of this!" My head started to ache. Maybe after all this was done, I could sleep for an entire day. I had earned it.

But first, I needed to think, so I sat down on the ground and the bottom of my backpack landed roughly behind me.

The kkwaenggwari.

With some renewed excitement, I extracted the gongs, wrapped in towels.

"Can we call her?" I asked.

Mom sighed. "You have a whole host of surprises in that bag of yours."

"Made sense to bring them, didn't it?"

"Okay, let's try." Mom nodded and reached for a gong.

"Same as last time, right?" I asked.

"Yes, same as last time. On three."

I held the kkwaenggwari by its string and got ready.

"One, two, three," Mom said as we both swung our mallets gently to strike our gongs.

The tone of the sound produced by the brass was powerful, filling the air quickly and sending little waves of air current all around me, almost enveloping me like the mist from the steam clock had.

It didn't take long for Halmeoni's face to appear in the gong again.

"Oh, look, I can see her again," Mom said with no enthusiasm.

Halmeoni was all smiles.

"Hi, Halmeoni! Are you okay? They freed you? Where are you?"

"Stephen, I'm fine. Calm down."

"Told you she'd be fine," Mom said.

"Can you come see us?" I asked.

"Why don't you come here?" she retorted.

"But where are you?"

"*The Great Sea is the place where we are free,*" she sang. "Come see me."

"Really! You were always the most unreasonable person. It's far easier for you to come see us than for us to pass through a giant rock!" Mom said bitterly.

"I want to see if he can." Halmeoni's eyes sparkled.

"Oh, not another one of her infuriating tests," Mom cried.

"I've already been to The Great Sea."

"By yourself," Halmeoni replied.

"How can I go without Abigail?"

"Hold the kkwaenggwari close to you. Feel it. Let your qi flow," she instructed. "Only the most powerful mudangs and baksu mudangs can cross realms."

"This is absurd," Mom muttered.

"He has everything he needs," Halmeoni said to Mom. "I believe he's ready."

Courage, I said to myself, closing my eyes and pressing the gong against my chest. *Brass brings courage.*

The gong pulsed gently against me, and I let it fill me with everything it had to offer. Not only courage but the heart of my ancestors, who had spoken to the spirits for generations before me . . . until my mother came along, anyway.

But there was something different too. Maybe it was my O'Driscoll side, maybe it was something else, but a feeling of longing filled me. A longing for a piventurate adventure — because it is who I am.

CHAPTER 29

I knew I could do it this time, and whether she liked it or not, Mom was coming with me. With the kkwaeng-gwari in our hands, what was going to stop us?

"We're going through that rock," I told her. "You and me. Together."

She looked up at the dark ceiling of The Midway, made up of dirt and small stones, before letting out a sigh of despair. "How?"

"You're not the most adventurous mudang, are you?"

"No, I am not." She shook her head.

"Always a big scaredy cat," Halmeoni chided. I stared down at her face in the gong I was pressing to my stomach. She had rotated herself so she was looking up at me.

"Take my hand. Trust me."

She grimaced and stuck out her clammy hand.

"I'll be waiting," Halmeoni said as she disappeared from the kkwaenggwari.

"Good, she isn't going to watch our failure in real time. I'd never hear the end of it."

"We're not going to fail," I said confidently.

Mom's face was filled with skepticism.

"Come on. How would you feel if you passed *through* the rock wall?" I asked.

She considered it for a moment. "Probably pretty pleased with myself, due to the impossibility of the task."

"They call it The Nexus."

She raised her eyebrows.

"I wasn't in charge of the names, okay? I'm just telling you facts." I squeezed her hand. "So, are you ready or what?"

Gripping my hand, she sighed heavily. "Well, I suppose the worst thing that could happen would be a broken bone or two."

"Hold the kkwaenggwari tight — feel it," I reminded her.

"Oh, believe me, I'm feeling it. It's the only thing between me and this giant rock!"

"No, the only thing between you and this rock is your attitude."

She looked off into the distance. "What a day. Scolded by both my son and my deceased mother. I am one lucky woman."

When did Mom turn into such a drama queen?

With a dip of my head, I signaled for her to get ready.

"Wait!" she yelled. "I need a moment!"

She squeezed her eyes shut. I felt the tension in her hand ease, which was good, because it was getting kind of damp and gross. Then her chest heaved, and she breathed in and out slowly.

"Release the tension and find your center."

She glared at me, and then resumed her attempt at self-relaxation.

"Okay," she said eventually, adjusting the kkwaeng-gwari in her hand.

"On three." I looked her straight in the eyes. "One, two, three!" We both started to run, although Mom's old legs needed a little extra tug. I held her hand tight and forced her to keep up. "Piventurates for life!" I yelled. Clasping our kkwaenggwari, we hurtled toward the rock . . . then we passed through and emerged, facing The Great Sea.

We skittered to a halt and pebbles flew around our feet. Mom had her eyes shut and reluctantly pried one open before realizing that we had done it. Finally, I had passed through The Nexus on my feet and with a little dignity!

"What just happened?" she asked, squinting.

"It's all good," I said, smiling and nodding at her. "We're still in one piece. This is The Great Sea!" Like a salesperson, I gestured broadly with an open palm.

"Hello!" Halmeoni rushed over to us.

I wished I could give her a hug. Finally, I was meeting my grandmother!

She was wearing a traditional Korean dress, a hanbok. It wasn't one of those fancy ones I've seen pictures of. It looked rustic and plain. Her form was shimmery, but the details of her face were clear. She seemed kinder now than she had the first time she'd appeared to me through the kkwaenggwari. Maybe it was because she was free.

"Wow, strong young boy!" Halmeoni floated around me to get a good look.

"You're far from home, Eomeoni," Mom said, tucking the kkwaenggwari under one arm.

"Not exactly on a vacation," she replied.

"Did they hurt you at all?" I asked.

"No, no. I'm fine."

"See?" Mom whispered to me.

I was quietly feeling quite pleased with myself — I'd just helped Willy *and* saved Halmeoni. My eyes locked with Halmeoni's and I realized I was sort of expecting her to look at me, you know, fondly. I did not expect her to start howling with laughter.

I frowned slightly.

Mom threw up her hands in exasperation. "How is this amusing?"

Halmeoni slowly composed herself. "I have a small confession."

My frown increased.

"What do you mean?" I asked.

"I wasn't trapped," she said sheepishly.

"What do you mean?" Mom repeated after me. The beginnings of an eyeball bulge started to emerge.

"Ah, I can't believe you fell for it," Halmeoni teased Mom. "How can they trap *me*?" She laughed at the idea.

"*What do you mean?*" Mom said again, louder this time. Eyeballs in full bulge mode.

"Those men, they look very nasty — the one with the face." She gestured to her cheek and did a cutting motion before she shivered. "But with one honorable purpose. Almost selfless. They wanted to help stop their captain from falling into The Chasm. Awful place."

Mom crossed her arms while I stood there like a frozen mannequin. I almost dropped my kkwaenggwari.

"And?" Mom said impatiently.

"They found me — they came a long way, really — and asked me to help give you motivation. I knew your powers were blooming." Halmeoni looked directly at me. "But thought maybe you would be afraid or worried."

Now I was crossing my arms too. The wrinkles in my forehead felt deeply etched.

"We talked. They asked, I helped." Halmeoni shrugged.

Mom's lips were in a full-on pucker now. "You tricked us?" Mom exploded.

"Not tricked! *Encouraged!*" Halmeoni defended herself.

Mom swiveled on the heels of her leather shoes and turned her back to Halmeoni while muttering, "Truly unbelievable! Even dead, she somehow manages to rile me up." Her arms gestured wildly. "This is exactly the reason I left Korea in the first place!"

"You played me," I finally said to Halmeoni, starting to fully realize what was happening.

"I *helped* you." She reached out to poke my shoulder. Her finger pressed against my shirt like a tickle.

I burst out laughing. Mom and I got *played*. It was hilarious. There I was, fretting about Halmeoni's trapped spirit, while she and Captain Sapperton's crew were plotting behind our backs on the best way to "motivate" me. They deserved my respect. All of them.

My sides ached and tears of laughter welled up in my eyes. Mom still paced like an angry lion, back and forth on the beach.

"Come on, Mom," I said, wiping a tear away. "It's kind of funny."

"I am not amused, Stephen." She stopped her angry striding and violently kicked at a pile of pebbles instead.

"Ah, never could take a joke. Come on. What do you think?" Halmeoni asked Mom, looking over her shoulder, staring out at the vast open space of The Great Sea. "It's very special for you to be here. You must look."

Mom gave her head a quick shake and puffed out a burst of air. She looked visibly calmer now. I think she managed to find her center!

"Do you hear them?" Halmeoni asked.

Mom nodded. I closed my eyes to listen carefully. The sound of the water lapping at the edge of the beach was, at first, the only thing I could hear. Then, finally, once I filtered out that sound, I could pick up voices much more clearly than the last time I was here: the quiet discussions, the laughter, the joy. I could hear it all but oddly, I couldn't *see* anyone.

"*The Great Sea is the place where we are free*," Halmeoni sang. "No spirit should be trapped. He was no angel, but he did not deserve The Chasm either. You did exactly the right thing by helping the captain."

Halmeoni was right. My eyes still closed, I beamed at the idea that I had done something good. The chatter of the ghosts was soothing and like a soft melody dancing in my ears.

The sound of Mom grumbling to herself made me open my eyes. When I looked out at the horizon, something caught my attention. "What's that?" I said as I peered across the water.

I held my hands up to shield my eyes and squinted to get a better view.

"It's a boat," I said to myself. "Or is it two boats?"

"Ah, good," Halmeoni approved.

"I don't see anything," Mom said, staring into the distance.

"How can you not see them?" I asked her. They were pretty obvious!

"Stephen, is that you?" A voice carried distinctly across the water.

Was that *Abigail* calling me — from one of the boats? I squinted harder.

Moving faster than I had thought possible, the boats became clearer. It couldn't be! But I'd recognize that dirty paint job anywhere! One of them was *Blackbeard's Vestige*, and flanking it, another ship I did not recognize.

It was larger than *Blackbeard's Vestige*, four-masted and definitely a galleon. The long skinny beakhead gave it away. This was a fast ship, suited for cargo and traveling long distances. Also a preferred ship of pirates.

"My ride home is here," Halmeoni said.

My head snapped in her direction. "What?"

But before Halmeoni could answer, Abigail flew off the deck of the ship and raced toward us. Within seconds, she was hovering before me with a gigantic smile on her face.

"Word spread very quickly that you were back! But how did you . . ." She gestured toward The Nexus. Abigail seemed surprised and confused. "I was expecting to see you in The Midway, not *here*! I thought that last time . . ."

"I did need you last time. But this time, I managed to summon a little courage." I showed her the kkwaeng-gwari. Something I noticed surprised me. "You're wearing my bandanna!" She had it tied around her neck like a scarf. I felt a small flush creep across my face.

"I was holding on to it, waiting for your return. You did say you'd return, after all. Do you want it back?"

"*Please* keep it," Mom said.

"Where are my manners? My name is Abigail Morris." She curtsied to Mom and Halmeoni. "You must be Stephen's family."

Mom and Halmeoni tipped their heads.

"You. Me. Here. Again. This is surprising." I laughed.

Abigail beamed. "Speaking of surprises." Her eyes darted to the two ships.

Mom was still squinting off into the distance. "What *are* you looking at? I don't see a ship!"

"Stop fooling around, Mom," I said testily. "I don't know the other one, but one of them you definitely saw moored at the marina, right?"

"I never fool around, Stephen. I don't see a single boat, never mind two." She gave me a very long look.

Then she closed her eyes and breathed in deeply, trying to channel whatever mudang energy she had in her. When she finally opened her eyes, I saw her staring intently at the sea.

"Oh my . . ." she said quietly.

"It's *Blackbeard's Vestige*. Right, Abigail?"

"It most certainly is!" Abigail confirmed.

"It was moored at Riverside Docks."

"It's a ghost ship, Stephen," Mom said.

"What? But I could see it! For over a week. At home. That's what I was staring out the window at!"

"How wonderful!" Halmeoni's spirit seemed to radiate. "You see, it's been building in you longer than you knew."

"I couldn't see it until now," Mom said, baffled. "And I needed to focus quite hard to do so."

"That's your own fault," Halmeoni reminded her.

After only just meeting my grandmother, I liked her. I liked her a lot.

"But there's a second ship," I said to Abigail. "I don't know that one. It's not familiar." Like *Blackbeard's Vestige*, it looked somewhat battered and rundown — but magnificent at the same time.

"It's *The Eidolon*," she replied, suppressing a grin.

"*The Eidolon*," I repeated slowly. "Captain Sapperton's ship?"

Abigail clapped and squealed. "He just told me *everything*! Oh, Stephen, you did a marvelous thing!"

I fixed my gaze on the two ships coming straight toward the beach. I counted six hazy figures standing on the deck of *The Eidolon*.

"Thank you, lad!" Captain Sapperton bellowed from behind the wheel. He floated over to the very edge of the beakhead and waved proudly. Because he was right where he belonged, he was luminescent. "We're off on an adventure across The Great Sea to the Pacific, and beyond! We might find a little trouble on the way — who knows!"

"Oy!" Sliced Cheek yelled to get my attention. I watched as he and the other crewmates saluted me. Dumbfounded, I returned the gesture as best I could.

"Okay, I have a long journey home. Traveling is very tiring," Halmeoni said, floating a few feet away toward *The Eidolon*.

Mom raised a finger and pointed wildly. "Wait, you're going on *their* ship?"

"How do you think I got here in the first place?" she asked.

My grandmother had hitched a ride from her home in The Vast Sea across the Pacific Ocean to The Great Sea — in a pirate ghost ship. She was more awesome than I could have imagined.

Halmeoni turned to Mom. "Take care of him." She looked at me. "Let him be who he is."

"I'm trying my best," Mom replied, looking irritated.

"Try harder!" Halmeoni said firmly.

"You're saying goodbye?" I asked. I wasn't ready.

"We'll see each other again. Don't you worry," Halmeoni said. "You cannot stay here long anyway."

She floated over to me and gently pointed to my arm. It was happening again. I was starting to fade away.

"Oh dear," Mom replied, looking at her fuzzy forearms.

"This is just the start of your adventure and your training. You know how to contact me." Halmeoni tenderly put her hand near the kkwaenggwari. "You have done your duty. This is what you were born to do, to listen and to help. You are doing a good job. I'm proud of you."

I couldn't take my eyes off her. When she looked at me, the gong buzzed slightly in my hands, and I knew that we had this thing between us now. Whatever it was, it had been hidden for too long (thanks, Mom), but now that it was discovered, I was *never* going to let it go.

Halmeoni put her hand up to my face, and I felt the misty touch of her fingers against my cheek. "I'll be watching you," she told me. The skirt of her hanbok swirled as she turned to leave, but she quickly spun back toward me and said, "But not in a creepy way."

CHAPTER 30

Halmeoni was on board *The Eidolon* in an instant.

"And that, Stephen, is your grandmother," Mom said humorlessly as soon as Halmeoni flew away.

"She's awesome."

The galleon maneuvered quickly to the port side, more agile than I could believe, and with the crew masterfully unfurling sails, swinging jibs, and pulling ropes, the ship sailed off into The Great Sea.

Abigail had stood quietly the whole time I had talked to my grandmother and while we watched *The Eidolon* sail away. And for the few moments I hadn't looked at it, *Blackbeard's Vestige* had come much closer to shore.

I also noticed the eerie quiet around us. It was as if the closer the ship came, the quieter The Great Sea was. I listened for whispers and conversation, and I heard nothing. *The Eidolon* was now only a dot on the horizon.

Abigail began to dance around me. "I simply cannot contain myself for a moment longer! I have the most amazing surprise. It was quite a rush to organize, but I would be very pleased for you to meet my . . ." She held up her fingers and silently counted. "I believe we're first cousins, four times removed? Or is it five? No matter! It is my pleasure to introduce you to Captain Edward Marino, the captain of *Blackbeard's Vestige*. He says he's been watching you for quite some time." Abigail's eyes twinkled mysteriously.

Why were people secretly and weirdly watching me all the time? Although feeling somewhat unnerved, I had to admit I was also bubbling with anticipation.

"How is it that these old wrecks are even here?" Mom asked.

"As you already know, The Great Sea is a rather special place. *The Great Sea is the place where we are free*," Abigail sang. "I was not entirely sure Captain Marino could sail here, being that . . ."

"We're not supposed to *be* here?" I finished her sentence.

"Yes," she agreed. "But the two of us managed to navigate our way, rather quickly in fact! While the ship itself may appear somewhat derelict, the captain of it is rather exceptional. I think he may make up for the condition of the boat."

My heart pounded in my chest. I waited for Abigail to tell me more.

"Like you, Captain Marino talks to ghosts."

Slowly, Mom's eyes drifted toward mine. I felt my bubble deflate a little. *Another* one like us? Was there a 50-percent-off sale at the local department store on the power to talk to ghosts? I felt decidedly less special than I had three minutes ago.

The two-masted brigantine I knew so well approached as close to shore as she dared. A man wearing a baseball cap, baggy plaid shorts, and a polo shirt came up to the rails and hollered, "All aboard!" His voice resonated forcefully through The Great Sea.

I was a bit thrown by his appearance. He looked nothing like a spiritual pirate. The plaid shorts especially — he seemed to have just come from a coffee shop. No jewelry!

No bandanna! No cutlass! What kind of pirate was he, anyway? Had he no respect for at least a *few* pirate traditions? I found myself frowning. This was all too confusing.

Abigail, who hadn't stopped grinning since spotting us, noticed my expression and looked puzzled. "Whatever is the matter, Stephen? I would have thought you'd be thrilled to meet Captain Marino!"

I hadn't realized how obvious my emotions were on my face.

Trying hard to recover, I said, "I'm really happy to meet him. I am!" I thought about Brandon, and I smiled — maybe a little too big. *He* could pull it off, but I wasn't sure I could, so I tried to tame the goofy grin a little.

"I'm just surprised that the captain, you know, talks to ghosts too." I paused, then asked, "How does a living man sail a ghost ship?"

She looked at me, bemused, and waited a moment before she answered. "How does a living boy talk to ghosts in the realm of the dead?" she asked.

I opened my mouth to argue but promptly closed it. She had a point, didn't she? Abigail smiled broadly and started to giggle.

"Great, a golfing pirate on a ghost ship," Mom said coldly as she stared at the boat.

"I said . . . *all aboard!*" Captain Marino thundered from the deck.

"Does he expect us to *swim*?" Mom asked, baffled.

In a sudden moment of inspiration, I swiveled on my heels to make sure that the old dory was still on the beach where I had left it. It was.

"That." I tapped Mom on the arm and drew her attention to the dory. I took the kkwaenggwari out of Mom's hand and started to wrap both of them up to put back into my backpack.

"Wasn't it bad enough you made me run through a rock? Now you want me to drown?" Mom looked up at the sky.

"It's seaworthy." I *hoped* it was seaworthy, anyway.

"Looks can certainly be deceiving," she replied, sighing.

Tell me about it.

I started to drag the boat into the water. Without being too obvious, I checked the bottom of the hull for any large holes. The inside of the boat was full of dead leaves and twigs, and I cleared it out as fast as I could. Luckily, there was a single old paddle sitting under the seats.

Mom looked down at her pointy, expensive-looking shoes. "These are ostrich!"

"Next time, you should wear something more practical!" Wearing fine ostrich-leather shoes to The Midway: ludicrous! Crocs: smart.

Mom scowled. "You're hardly one to give *fashion* advice!" She stared directly at my bandanna.

"*Humph!* Get in," I said, undeterred, tossing my bag into the boat.

Mom looked at her shoes again. Deciding they were too nice to get wet, she took them off and threw them into the dory. Barefooted, she stepped gingerly onto the pebbly beach. She adjusted the strap of her small purse before getting into the boat. Then she picked up her shoes and sat reluctantly on the bench.

With a mighty heave, I pushed the dory the rest of the way into the water and jumped inside. Abigail floated alongside.

"There's only one paddle," Mom said, looking around. She held her shoes tight to her chest.

"I'll do it," I told her as I picked it up. There wasn't really a proper handhold, but how hard could it be?

I dipped the paddle into the water and propelled the boat forward — slowly. Was Mom made of lead? Gah!

She was heavy. I grunted on my next stroke. Seemed like I had my answer. Paddling was *hard*. While I liked all boats in general, boats with diesel engines were definitely higher up on my list than boats that required manual labor.

"We haven't got all day!" Captain Marino bellowed. Did he have a quiet inside voice, I wondered, or was his only volume barking and yelling?

"I'm surprised he can talk to the spirits. I don't get that sense from him," Mom said, looking at him critically.

"You didn't get that sense from me either, remember?" I snorted.

She gave me her I'm-going-to-ignore-that face. My arms were starting to burn.

"Doesn't look much like a pirate, does he?" Mom observed.

Gee, thanks, Mom — I hadn't noticed. Everything she said was so annoying right now. I rolled my eyes, which was hard to do when paddling against her dead weight.

Abigail piped up. "He does seem rather casually dressed, I suppose, but make no mistake: He is a first-class sailor, and he has the biggest piventurate heart you could imagine." I shot her a look as soon as she said "piventurate," and she winked.

"It's not a word," Mom said flatly.

"No, it's a *spirit*." Abigail paused before she broke out into giggles.

I wanted to keep paddling, but I couldn't. I was laughing too hard.

"I see what you did there," Mom replied. I think even she was suppressing a smile.

"Hurry it up!" Captain Marino shouted. We were closer to *Blackbeard's Vestige* now — close enough for me to see his face. Clean-shaven! No twirly mustache! His hair did look a little scruffy sticking out the back of his cap, but not long enough for a braid of any kind.

Mom chuckled to herself.

"What's so funny?" I asked her as I struggled to resume paddling.

"Well, I was just thinking about Captain Marino's name. As you probably guessed, Marino is derived from the Latin word *marinus*, or 'of the water.'"

No, Mom, I hadn't guessed that at all. I grunted as I put all my weight into each stroke.

When I didn't answer, Mom continued, "He's the captain of a ship. *Of the water.* Understand?" Mom said this in a way that made me feel like one of her students.

"Yes, Mom." I gritted my teeth.

"Sometimes people are just born with or given a name that suits them," she replied. "Or perhaps they become something because of their name. It's fascinating, isn't it?"

"What does Stephen mean?" Abigail asked her.

Mom was really in her element now. She explained, "It's derived from the Greek meaning *wreath* or *crown* and by extension, in Ancient Greece, the winner of a contest was often given a wreath to wear around their head."

I snorted. "What contest have I ever won?"

"The first boy to ever set sail in The Great Sea, obviously!" Abigail laughed.

"That's not *really* a contest," I told her.

"It's an achievement nonetheless!" Abigail said.

Mom pondered a little longer. "Actually, the Greek word for Stephen encapsulates a few other ideas besides being the winner of a contest. I think more appropriately it also suggests *honor*."

I liked that. I liked that a lot.

"Names can be very meaningful on many levels." She then paused again but had that look like she wasn't quite done lecturing. "For instance, the Korean Oh clans are descended from the Wu clans of China, which are attributed to starting the Chinese Navy."

"Wait, wait." I stopped paddling. "So, I come from a line of mudangs *and* sailors?" I almost jumped out of the dory. *Now* she was talking!

"Well, my ancient history is a little rusty but yes, I believe that is correct."

"Seems that Stephen is doing just what he ought to be doing." Abigail looked delighted.

"But I'm only half Oh. Don't forgot my O'Driscoll side," I said. "Do you know what O'Driscoll means?"

"It's probably Celtic for absentee father," Mom said scornfully, looking away. She scratched her neck.

"Hurry up and paddle harder! Are you even trying? The day isn't going to wait for you!" Captain Marino yelled from the deck.

"Aye aye, Captain!" I replied loudly as I tried to refocus on the task in front of me.

Giving it everything I had, I resumed paddling and after just a few more strokes, we were close enough for Captain Marino to unfurl a rope ladder down the side of his ghost ship.

We coasted up to the side of *Blackbeard's Vestige* and I reached over to grab the rope. I was half expecting my hand to pass right through it, but the rope felt solid enough. The dory steadied and I said to Mom, "You go first." Not because I was scared or anything, but because I had good manners. Ladies first, right?

Her eyes tracked up the length of the rope to where Captain Marino was waiting with his elbows leaning on the gunwale.

Mom slipped her shoes back on and sighed as the dory swayed gently beneath us. She gathered herself to a shaky standing position, grabbed the rope, and began her climb. "This is *not* how I imagined I'd be ending my day," she grumbled to herself.

I let her get up a few rungs before I started, just to give us some space. Nobody needs to be that up-close-and-personal with their mother's butt.

After grunting and complaining all the way up the rope, Mom was finally near the top. The ladder was only eight rungs high, as this was a small brigantine. Imagine if it had been a full-sized vessel! The footing was awkward because the weight of my body caused the rope to give way slightly each time I climbed a rung. The ladder was also extremely dirty. A fine sailor he may have been, but a good cleaner he was not.

Abigail hovered alongside me and asked, "Are you doing all right?"

"Well," I said reaching for the next rung, "the view is . . . unpleasant." I gestured to Mom's behind.

Abigail sniggered.

"I heard that," Mom said, without looking at me.

Captain Marino reached out his hand. "Welcome aboard!" He hauled Mom over the side. Gracelessly, she tumbled onto the deck.

I looked down to the water and watched the dory drift away.

Abigail said, "I'll meet you up top," and she floated upward and disappeared from my sight. Captain Marino silently watched me and when our eyes met, I hesitated. Wrapping my right elbow around the rope to steady myself, I pushed my bandanna forward on my brow and made sure the knot was secure. I puffed out a short breath.

My stomach fluttered violently. This was it. Soon, I would be aboard a real pirate ghost ship.

CHAPTER 31

"**S**tephen Oh-O'Driscoll." Captain Marino put his hands on his hips and eyed me up and down. "My cousin has told me a lot about you. Nice to finally meet you in person. Welcome aboard *Blackbeard's Vestige.*"

"Thank you, sir!" My voice cracked. I saluted him as it was the proper thing to do.

The fresh air on the deck brushing my arms felt like a force 2 on the Beaufort scale: gentle breeze.

Captain Marino turned to Abigail and nodded. "You were right, he'll do fine." Then speaking directly to me, he said, "I'd been hoping for quite some time that you'd come see me aboard my boat when I was moored, but the last time I saw you, you just sort of disappeared. You're not a ghost too, are you?" He chuckled.

I remembered hiding from him, and immediately my armpits went into hyper-hydration mode.

"When an old seadog pirate like me sees a boon companion, well . . . I just knew we had to meet."

"Who says 'boon companion'?" Mom muttered to herself.

"But you don't *look* like a seadog or a pirate!" I blurted out. "You're wearing plaid shorts!"

I regretted my words instantly. Didn't Willy tell *me* that I didn't look like pirate material, and here I was telling Captain Marino the *exact* same thing? It would have served me right if a giant albatross had come swooping by and hit me square on the head with a fresh load.

Instead of being offended, Captain Marino just burst out laughing.

I stole a glance over at Mom. She squeezed a dollop of sanitizing gel into her hands and rubbed vigorously.

"Have you ever worn leather breeches, Stephen? Not comfortable. They leave nothing to the imagination. Now these? This is comfort!" He snapped the elastic of his waistband.

I puckered my lips together and I looked down at my own feet. Okay, Crocs didn't exactly scream fearless explorer, I admit. With my toes curled up inside my shoes, I had to concede that comfort was important.

"Maybe you were expecting a captain that looked like one of those cartoonish characters from movies, but those men aren't the real thing."

"What *is* the real thing, then?" I asked.

"A pirate is a unique soul. A tenacious wanderer. A daring innovator."

With each description, I found myself slowly nodding in agreement. Eat your heart out, *Cambridge Dictionary*. *This* was the proper definition of *pirate*.

He continued. "A person who takes chances. Even with their wardrobe." Captain Marino snickered. "Now, I have a question for *you*."

"Yes?" I replied nervously.

"As you can see, I really could use some help around here. It's not an easy task finding the right crew for a ship like this. With your mother's permission, will you accept the job as first mate of *Blackbeard's Vestige*?"

Abigail started darting around excitedly. Mom slapped her forehead.

In my daydreams, I had learned to sail on an actual ship, not a ghost ship, but hey, sometimes it's important to just go with the flow. I felt my knees go weak, but

I straightened myself up as quickly as I could. I glanced at Mom. She rolled her eyes and looked away but gave a slight nod of the head.

I responded, "Aye, it would be my honor, Captain."

The captain dipped his head slightly and then hollered, "Anchor up!" before walking toward the helm.

Was he talking to me? I had so many questions I wanted to ask, like *Why does a ghost ship need an anchor?* But the captain's orders had interrupted my thoughts.

I must have looked confused because he then said, "Yes, Stephen, even ghost ships must be sailed! I can't just say to it 'head east' and have it *magically* steer itself." He pointed to the stern with one hand, and with the other, he held the large wooden steering wheel that was varnished to a glossy shine and possibly the cleanest thing on the entire ship.

I threw my backpack on the deck before I ran to the back of the boat to find the rope that had the anchor tied to it. "Now what?" I yelled.

"You pull!" he shouted back.

While I hauled the dirty, wet rope out of the water, Abigail hovered near Captain Marino, and Mom wiped down a bench before taking a seat.

"Surprisingly, it feels real," Mom said as she sat.

"Why don't I just fall right through?" She looked at Captain Marino, waiting for an answer.

"Who's to say what is real and what is not? Just because you can't see something doesn't mean it's not there, and just because you see something doesn't mean it is." He gripped the ship's wheel.

She gave him the kind of stare where her forehead and her nose wrinkled deeply.

As I turned my attention to the task of pulling a slimy rope out of the water, the same thought kept spinning around in my mind — *How was this even happening?* I was glad to have a job to distract me.

Methodically, the rope emerged over the top of the gunwale and as it did, the captain's Jolly Roger, the replica of Blackbeard's flag, started to catch the wind. I remembered *my* Jolly Roger, in my backpack.

"Oy!" Captain Marino said loudly. "Why isn't that anchor up yet?"

"On it, sir!" I finished hauling it on deck. Before me lay a wet pile of rope and one barnacle-encrusted anchor.

"Good work! Now let's feel the wind lashing at our faces and get you home."

"We're going home?" I was caught off guard. "Can we get home this way? I thought we could only go back through the steam clock!" I lay down on the deck, trying to catch my breath.

"You think there's only one way back?" Captain Marino laughed and slapped his thigh. "Ah, so naive." He shook his head, amused.

I glanced over at Mom. She seemed to have the deep wrinkles of consternation creased permanently into her nose. "There's another way?" she asked quietly.

"There's *always* another way," Captain Marino answered with a wink.

Mom looked startled.

"If you'd taken some time to explore the world with a little more, shall we say, *enthusiasm*, you'd have found out that there is much more to see. But one must be willing to look." He stared at Mom with the slightest of smirks. She busied herself, straightening her shirt.

Captain Marino knew his stuff. He knew more than Mom.

"How long have you known you were a baksu?" I asked him breathlessly as I sat up.

"Huh? What's a baksu?"

"He's not going to know the word," Mom said. "Try 'spiritual medium.'"

"Okay, Captain, how long have you been a spiritual medium?"

"That's funny." His shoulders gently rocked from holding in his laughter.

Feeling very puzzled by his response, I tilted my head and stared at him.

"You're the captain of a ghost ship. You can talk to Abigail!" I said, frustrated. Even a first mate can be annoyed by his captain. "How is that funny?"

"You make it seem all hocus-pocus." He danced his fingers in the air.

"But you're alive!" I stood up.

"So are you!" Captain Marino replied quickly.

"Yes, but I'm a baksu."

"Excellent point, Stephen," Mom said. My back straightened and my chest puffed out. She was not easy to impress. "I haven't been thinking rationally since my son forced me to run through a giant wall of rock, but come to think of it, it *is* most strange that you are here." She looked Captain Marino up and down before standing to join us.

"She's a mudang but trying hard not to be," I explained to the captain as I pointed to Mom. She made a sour face.

Captain Marino wrinkled his forehead. "Well, I really don't know what the big deal is. This ship once belonged to Abigail's grandfather. I believe he won it in a high-stakes card game."

Cool. Wide-eyed and mouth agape, I looked at Abigail, who smiled shyly.

Captain Marino continued, "It's a family heirloom of sorts, isn't it? It's my duty to keep sailing it. Because we're family, her mother has been visiting me for quite some time. She likes to check in and make sure I'm doing well."

"Mother *is* a very caring person," Abigail whispered to me.

"As for being here, well, none of us breathing types really should be in this realm. Have you noticed?" He looked down at his arm, causing me to look down at mine. We were all fading. I was a bit less solid than I had been just minutes before. "I tend to navigate through the waters of the living. I just made a special trip here at the request of my relation. It's my first time here. It's hard to say no to family, isn't it?"

I glared at Mom.

"So, the spirits come to you? You hear them? And you see them?" Mom pressed the captain for more details.

Captain Marino stuck his bottom lip out to think. "Well, no. Only Abigail and her mother so far."

"The spirits are all around, not just in places like The Midway and The Great Sea. Some journey to places for the living, like Rail's End," Abigail said.

Oh, I knew all about that.

Abigail continued, "There are some living who are more receptive to listening to us than others. Most of the living don't hear or see us, though. Captain Marino has always been a generous, open person, so it makes communicating with him easy."

It was just like Dad being able to hear Halmeoni without realizing it was a spirit talking to him.

"All this *spooky* chatter is giving me the chills." The captain playfully danced his fingers in the air again.

For some reason, Mom looked relieved. "Ah, so not a true baksu. But a person only lightly connected to the spirits. Those people are much more common."

Captain Marino stared at Mom with the faintest trace of a crooked smile, and his expression caused her to look away immediately. But it was hard to miss the flush on her cheeks.

CHAPTER 32

Being in a pirate ghost ship in the middle of The Great Sea was pretty awesome. It felt just as good as the last time I'd sailed on *The Climb* — maybe even better. The wind whipping at my clothes, the sudden spray of saltwater, the slight nausea — it all felt so *right*. But I knew this journey was special; The Great Sea wasn't where I belonged. *Blackbeard's Vestige* was bringing me home from a job I needed to do. Now that I had done that job, I had to return to the land of the living.

Behind us, the shore where Mom and I had launched the dory grew smaller. I could hardly make it out anymore. *Blackbeard's Vestige* sailed confidently and with speed.

As I sat on the deck and breathed deeply, I realized there had been a question bubbling inside me and I couldn't keep it in anymore.

"Sir!" I scrambled to attention and stood stiffly in front of the captain. "I have a request, as your first mate!"

"Out with it, boy!" he bellowed.

I hesitated before I finally asked, "May I fly my Jolly Roger?" My stomach turned waiting for his reply.

"You've got your own Jolly Roger?" he asked, surprised. "Let's see it, then."

I scurried to my backpack and found my flag. I unfolded it to show him.

Holding it in my trembling hands, I worried it was silly.

"Is that one of my *napkins*?" Mom peered at it and then shot me a death stare.

I flashed her my teeth in a clenched smile.

"Tell me the story," Captain Marino ordered.

I cleared my throat and held the flag up against my chest. I had used a bottle of white correction fluid to draw my designs. It's *very* difficult to draw carefully with that stuff. You try it. I needed to explain my pictures. "Well, these two figures represent me and my best friend, Brandon." I turned to Abigail. "You'd like him."

Her gentle smile urged me to continue. "And these are cutlasses," I explained as I pressed my finger to the image. They kind of looked like bananas. I glanced nervously at Mom. "We're not so good at sword fighting yet. We're still working on it." Uncomfortable thoughts of Brandon's chipped teeth crept into my mind, and I felt my energy draining.

"That goes without saying," Mom said, rolling her eyes.

"Let the boy finish," Captain Marino scolded her. The stunned look on her face was priceless and buoyed me enough to finish my explanation.

I moved my finger to the top left corner of the flag. "This is a red sun, like a rising sun. Like heading off into a new day and not knowing what's around the corner." The red marker had not colored over the correction fluid as deeply as I would have liked.

My face felt so hot that I was sure I could roast a marshmallow on it.

Captain Marino looked at my Jolly Roger very intently, and with the slightest of nods, he said, "Very well, Stephen. You have my permission to fly your flag. You may use the flagpole located at the stern."

Abigail gasped with delight.

"Thank you, sir." I felt like I must be glowing.

"Isn't he the most generous of captains?" Abigail gushed.

I studied how the captain's Jolly Roger was attached to the pole and I knew immediately that I was going to have a problem.

My "flag" was a dinner napkin. There was no way to secure it. I had to get creative.

"You don't have safety pins, do you?" I asked Captain Marino.

"Of course I do! Lift up the bench there." He motioned to the bow. "A good sewing kit comes in handy when you've given yourself a nasty gash." He smiled as he stuck out his calf to show me a crooked scar.

I retrieved the box and picked through it until I found two safety pins. Then I headed back to the stern, ready to detach the pole from its base. The whole thing came apart easily. Using the two pins, I fastened my Jolly Roger to the bottom edge of Captain Marino's flag, which was still attached to the pole.

The symbol of the old pirate way — a copy of Blackbeard's original Jolly Roger — and mine, a symbol of the new way — the piventurate way. The two flags were connected.

This was epic.

When I finished remounting the flagpole and witnessed the two Jolly Rogers flapping together in the wind, the sound of their fluttering struck me as one of the purest things I had ever heard.

I watched them for a moment before Captain Marino barked, "Oy! Come to the wheel!"

With hardly a moment to enjoy the sight of my flag hanging properly from a pirate ship, my heart danced in my chest, and I sprinted to join him. He was going to let me *steer*!

"Take it," he told me.

The spoked steering wheel was large and imposing, but the first mate's job is to always obey the captain's orders, so I had no choice but to reply, "Aye aye, Captain!"

As he stepped away, I reached for the wheel. The spokes felt smooth and warm. The wheel seemed real to my hands and I held on tight. *Blackbeard's Vestige* was under my command. I gazed out at the calm waters of The Great Sea, and even though I hadn't slept properly in days, I had never felt so contented and relaxed. Everything about this moment felt perfect. Except there was one thing I needed to know.

"Sir?" I barked. There was something about being on this ship — suddenly even *I* was barking everything.

Captain Marino looked over his shoulder. "Yes?"

My voice dropped. "Do you ever think of yourself as a piventurate?"

He considered me for a moment before he replied, "Always."

"Me too," I replied with a grin. "Me too."

CHAPTER 33

The ship sailed smoothly for quite some time before Mrs. Morris appeared. Seeing her reminded me that the other spirits seemed to have vanished. I could barely hear them, and I definitely couldn't see them.

"Hello, Stephen!"

"Hi!" I was glad to see her again.

"This is your mother, I presume?" Mrs. Morris said pleasantly, looking at Mom.

I elbowed Mom and she finally waved a hello.

"Captain!" Mrs. Morris turned to her relation. "You are looking well."

"Thank you, cousin!" He bowed slightly.

"Lad, you've done a wondrous thing. It's the talk of The Great Sea. The others do nothing but prattle on about you and how you came back to help Captain Sapperton." She smiled. "Seeing him on board *The Eidolon*, well, it almost brought a tear to my eye."

"But where *are* all the other spirits?" I asked. "When we first got here, I could hear voices, but it's gone quiet. Really quiet!"

Captain Marino stepped next to me, and I handed him back the wheel.

Mom perked up. "You're right, I heard them at the start, but now they've all gone away."

"Oh, they're a little ... perturbed. Now, don't take this the wrong way, but *one* live one they could tolerate. However, *three* of you, well ... many of them think it's rather presumptuous of you to be here in our realm."

Mom and I glanced at each other uneasily.

"But I've had many spirits cross over and come bother me over the years. Sometimes in my own home," Mom argued.

"Yes, dear, and you've been rather rude to them, haven't you?" Mrs. Morris replied.

Abigail and I sniggered quietly.

"When we want your help, we'll ask. When we ask, do try to take us seriously," Mrs. Morris told me and Mom.

"Don't worry, I will," I assured her. Mom kept quiet.

"Abigail, dear, it's time," Mrs. Morris said gently.

"Already?"

"Yes, my love." Mrs. Morris pointed ahead to the horizon, where dense clouds seemed to hover on top of the water.

Abigail pouted before she said, "All right, Mother, just give me a moment, please."

Mrs. Morris turned to me. "Goodbye, Stephen. I'm sure we'll see you again. You should be right proud of yourself. Captain Sapperton was a lost soul, just too proud for his own good. But he's free now and that is because of *you*. But I do suspect that he'll be back soon. Cedar Coast is home, after all."

Home. I guess that was where everybody always wanted to be after a good adventure. I totally understood that.

Mrs. Morris dipped her head. I waved, and in an instant, she disappeared.

Abigail hovered beside me.

"It's time for me to say goodbye as well."

My heart dropped like a sinking ship. "Goodbye?" I exclaimed. "But . . ." I had just assumed, or hoped, that she'd come with us.

"I needed to be here with you — for now. Because the sea is wide, and the spaces between where the living and the dead coexist are tangled like the most difficult knot. I just wanted to make sure Captain Marino, expert sailor that he is, could find the way. Once we reach the right place, I will leave. In fact, we're almost there." She glanced at the thickening clouds. "You remember what I told you?" she asked the captain.

"Yes, I can see it — just up ahead. Where The Great Sea meets the world of the living," Captain Marino replied.

I squinted to try to see what he saw. There. I could see it. A spot where the horizon flickered. The slight haze of The Great Sea gave way to clearer sky. I turned to Abigail.

"But . . ." I sputtered. I couldn't find any words, even though there were so many things I wanted to say.

"I'll miss you too, Stephen," Abigail said shyly.

"I . . . I really wanted you to meet Brandon!" I was distressed.

"Oh, I think I will, one day. But I belong here for now. With my mother and the others."

"Could you come see me?"

"You wouldn't find it strange?"

"No! Not at all."

"All right, then. While mother does visit our local relations occasionally, she usually doesn't approve of ghosts who go and bother the living with their troubles."

"But you won't be bothering me," I assured her.

"Then maybe I'll pay you a visit in a fortnight. Until then, I have this to remember you by." She touched the bandanna she was wearing around her neck.

"I suppose I could always come see you in The Midway too," I told her. "It's easy-peasy. The steam clock at noon."

"Yes, you could, but . . ." She pointed to my disappearing hand.

Oh no — it was getting worse and worse.

Abigail floated closer to me. "This place isn't for the living. You need to go and *live*. You helped Willy. You've done your part. It's time for you to go home."

She reached out. My hand went quickly to the top of my head, and I took off my bandanna before I reached for her hand too. That familiar feeling, from every time she had touched me before, skipped across my fingers — a feeling that there was something between us. As a baksu, it only made sense that I was connected to all ghosts, but Abigail most of all.

I began to tie the second bandanna around her wrist. I knew she didn't need it. She already had one to remember me. But I wanted her to have it. I looked at her now, with the bandanna around her neck and now the second one around her wrist.

"Double Bandannas would be a great pirate name," I told her, as I rubbed the top of my head. As soon as I said it, my face ignited. "Kind of like our in-joke." I wanted to dig my way out of my embarrassment but was failing.

"Good friends always need something between them that only they understand," she said. "Abigail 'Double Bandannas' Morris. I shall be the envy of The Great Sea." She looked at her wrist and her eyes wrinkled in the corners. "A great friend of Double O Stephen, a great *piventurate* name. I hope that you remember that."

"My dad calls me that," I said quietly.

She smiled gently. "It's a good name."

I had finished tying the knot long before I let go of her wrist. She felt almost solid, and she left me with a glowing warmth on my hands.

"Now I think I'll go have a chat with my mother about Gramps. She shouldn't have held it against him all these years that he loved the sea. He wasn't really a pirate, anyway — more like a piventurate. I should like to see him again." Abigail turned and gave me a final grin.

Then she was gone.

CHAPTER 34

Captain Marino expertly steered his boat so it glided easily into the slip. With the gentlest of thumps, the boat hit the bumpers placed along the edge of the dock, he cut the engine, and we were home.

"You'll come sailing with me again, of course," Captain Marino announced.

I looked at Mom for approval. She rolled her eyes and looked away. It wasn't exactly a resounding yes, but it also wasn't a no!

I nodded vigorously. "What are you doing next weekend?"

"Teaching you to use a cutlass," he replied.

Mom's jaw flopped open.

Captain Marino reached into a wooden box on deck and said, "Relax, they're plastic." He lifted one large plastic cutlass out of the box to show Mom.

"That's a step up from branches," I told him. "Can I bring a friend? He's got the piventurate spirit too!" Brandon was going to *love* this.

"Hmm, I don't know," Captain Marino said, unsure.

"But we have this thing!" I started to panic.

"What thing?"

I felt embarrassed saying our oath in front of him and Mom. But I needed to show Captain Marino who Brandon was before Brandon missed out on this chance.

"We have the Piventurate's Oath," I told him.

"Really?" Mom said, dismayed.

"It's like the code we live by," I mumbled. "Or want to live by, at least."

"Let's hear it, then," Captain Marino said sharply.

I cleared my throat before I started.

We draw no blood
We play as one
We never give up
'Cause quitting's no fun

We keep our word
We are best mates
Piventurates for life
Adventure is our fate

I felt all nervous and worried by the last line. Would he accept Brandon on board?

"So, it's adventure you're after, is it?" Captain Marino inquired.

"Well, I'm not *after* it. It just seems to come my way," I explained.

"No traditional piracy, then?"

"No, I don't want to *rob* people."

"A young man of strong moral fiber." He pressed his lips together.

"So, can Brandon join us?" I asked hopefully.

"The more, the merrier," Captain Marino replied decisively.

"Really?" I was relieved.

"Any young sailor who lives by a code like that is welcome aboard."

"I outrank him, though, right?"

"Yes, Stephen, you may order him around."

I did a fist pump.

Mom stood up and craned her neck to look at the back of her pants. They were filthy. Ghost ships can collect a surprising amount of dirt.

"Thank you for the ride home, Captain," Mom said, hopelessly brushing her pants with her hands.

"I suppose we'll need to exchange phone numbers so we can decide when Stephen and his friend come by the ship." His eyes twinkled and he gave her the quickest of winks.

The color drained from her face.

Captain Marino began tapping into his phone. I peered over his shoulder. He had written "*Edgy Spirit Lady (Stephen's mom)*" as her name in the contact information. He passed the phone to Mom.

"Edgy Spirit Lady!" she sputtered, looking offended.

I reached over and put the number in myself.

"I didn't say *edgy* was bad. I kind of like edgy," Captain Marino said mischievously, tucking his phone back into his pocket.

"Well . . . Goodbye!" Mom made a beeline for the rope ladder. She unfurled it and hauled herself over the edge.

I saluted Captain Marino. "Well done, sir."

"I will see you soon, and I look forward to meeting your friend." He returned the salute. "Tie up the boat before you leave!" He tossed a length of rope over the side.

It was time to go home.

When you're tired and hungry, there is only one meal that makes sense. While not the most nutritious of foods, a nice package of instant ramen is sometimes just what you need.

I preferred the extra spicy kind, with the rooster on fire as its logo. If my face didn't melt while I was eating it, what was the point? Mom liked the really bland flavors.

"I don't like to gamble with my intestinal tract," she told me while emptying her packet of very plain broth powder into the pot. "That level of spice is not natural." She eyed my chosen package suspiciously.

While waiting for the noodles to cook, Mom went to clean herself up and I sat down at my desk and turned on my computer.

The last few days had been an overload of information. I was a baksu who could talk to spirits — even help them! Bonus, I was also well on my way to living the piventurate dream. Regular trips on *Blackbeard's Vestige* were in my future, and I was soon to become a decent sailor. I gave my head a rub. I missed my bandannas a little, but they were in good hands.

There was still one more thing that I wanted to know. I needed to look up "O'Driscoll."

I just about fell out of my seat when this page came up:

> The surname derives from the given name
> Eidirsceol, referring to a person who was
> alive in the early- to mid-tenth century. The
> word itself, eidirsceol, means "go-between"
> or "bearer of news." The O'Driscolls were,
> in general, a seafaring people of the coast.

Whoa. I wondered if Dad knew anything about this! I needed to talk to someone immediately. There was only one person who came to mind.

I messaged Brandon.

Wanna ride on pirate ship?

Huh? UR back! Early?!

Yup

Did it work? Willy? Grandma ok?

👍👍

👋

What do u mean ride on pirate ship?

Can u sleep over tonite? 2 much 2 tell u

Wait . . .

Mom says k

Meet at marina 1 hr?

AYE AYE!

I was positive Brandon was going to be able to see the ship. After all, he *had* felt the tattooed ghost's presence at school. He was a true believer, and there was no reason why he couldn't be a little something like Captain Marino. He would also definitely want to get some proper lessons on how to handle a cutlass. Maybe Brandon wasn't a baksu like me, but Abigail said that anyone open to communicating with the spirits probably could. I had never been more positive about anything in my life.

I glanced at the clock. Maybe I could go introduce Brandon to Captain Marino later. But the person I most wanted to introduce my best *living* friend to was Abigail. My new best *ghostly* friend would be back to see me soon, and I was going to make the introduction happen. I touched the pair of kkwaenggwari I had put on my bedside table, in the spot where *Treasure Island* used to be.

I powered down my computer and looked out the window at *Blackbeard's Vestige*. My Jolly Roger was flapping steadily in the breeze, and it was an awesome sight. The flag was just where it ought to be.

There was just one little thing I needed to add to my flag. Abigail would stand — I mean, *float* — alongside the image of me and Brandon. But I probably should consider attaching it more securely to the flagpole. I didn't want it to fly away in the wind the next time we went sailing. That would ruin the adventure.

My name is Stephen Oh-O'Driscoll. I just needed a bit of courage to realize that, as the first baksu-piventurate of Cedar Coast, it is the perfect name for me.

ACKNOWLEDGMENTS

I wish I had a great story about how I came up with the idea for this book, but truthfully, it's rather dull. One day, while wondering what I was going to write next, I started to think about the steam clock (designed and built by Raymond Saunders) located in Vancouver's Gastown district, and that was it. The first nugget of the story was born. I even dragged my kids to Gastown one day so we could look at it and I could start imagining it into a story. Then I had to write the darn thing.

Six difficult and substantial rewrites later, I can't even recall how pirates, ghosts, and mudangs got all tangled up with the steam clock in the first place.

I am once again reminded that producing a novel is hardly an individual effort. I have many people to thank.

A very big thank you to my sensitivity readers, Ann Doyon and Stacey Parshall Jensen, for virtually holding my hand and letting me know that I handled things as well as I could have. Archaa Shrivastav, for reminding me that sometimes the seemingly benign is often not so. Any mistakes or ill-conceived errors in judgement contained in the final draft of this story are entirely my own. I know I still have a lot to learn, and I am always willing to listen and try to do better.

Thanks to Leah Hong for taking the time to read and comment on an early draft. Apparently, you can meet an author-illustrator at the local swimming pool when your kids are taking lessons together. It is truly an epic origin story of finding friends in the most unexpected places.

Naomi and Laura, who provided early editorial feedback, thank you!

I am lucky to have an agent who is a calming presence in the frequently unsteady waters of publishing. Thank you, Laurel Symonds!

How could I not thank the team at Tundra/Penguin Random House Canada for generally being awesome?

Lynne Missen is a patient editor, and I am grateful for her guidance. I can't even begin to tell you how much better she makes my books. There are lots of you who work behind the scenes and don't actually ever speak to me, but I see you. I know you help get my books out into the world (and make them look really pretty too) and I send to you, across the country, many, many Korean finger hearts.

For once, my daughter willingly read one of my stories before it became an official bound book, and she asked good questions which made me go back and rethink parts of the story. Thank you, my sweet baby!

My nephews, Julian and Nicholas, for . . . well, you know.

Erin Joo for the front cover. It's everything I could have hoped for, yet so much more. I appreciate your talent and creativity!

A great hearty appreciation goes out to my local library for supplying me with books to learn all about sailing, boats, nautical flags, and pirates. I was hoping to visit a local sailing club and get firsthand experience, but then, you know, COVID happened.

This is important to me to mention. I've only scraped the surface of all the rituals and rich traditions, taking just bits and pieces of Korean shamanism to suit my story. Please be aware that there is so much more to know about mudangs and baksu mudangs that I haven't even begun to talk about in this book. If you are curious, there are many great online sources for you to learn more.

Because they are mentioned in the book, I ate a lot of spicy ramen and Korean fried chicken as food authenticity research. Just kidding, I just like to eat. But please note, eating spicy ramen can cause gastric distress when you are older than forty (trust me), so please enjoy it when you are young.

Author's warning: once you discover fried chicken the Korean way, you can never go back to the regular stuff. I'm not kidding. Fried chicken is no joking matter.